THE
demon
notebook

eRika mcgann

J
FICTION
MCGANN

sourcebooks
jabberwocky

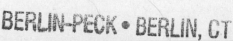

Published by Sourcebooks Jabberwocky, an imprint of Sourcebooks, Inc.
P.O. Box 4410, Naperville, Illinois 60567-4410
(630) 961-3900
Fax: (630) 961-2168
www.jabberwockykids.com

Originally published in 2012 in Ireland by The O'Brien Press Ltd.

Library of Congress Cataloging-in-Publication data is on file with the publisher.
Source of Production: Versa Press, East Peoria, Illinois, USA
Date of Production: April 2014
Run Number: 5001365

Printed and bound in the United States of America.
VP 10 9 8 7 6 5 4 3 2 1

For my dad,
who would be proud

contents

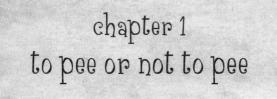

chapter 1
to pee or not to pee

"Two minutes!" whispered Grace Brennan, cradling her watch in her hand.

"Quiet, Grace!" said Ms. Lemon, whipping around to point at her with a marker.

"Sorry, Miss."

Grace kept her eyes down until she was sure the teacher had returned to the whiteboard. When the coast was clear, she quickly mouthed "one minute" to her friends and they all turned their attention to the boy sitting third from the left in the front row. Grace kept her eyes on his back, trying to picture him leaping out of his chair and bounding out of the room. Glancing back at her watch, she held out her fingers to count down from five, four, three, two, one…

Nothing.

The girls held their concentration for a few more moments.

Still nothing.

Andrew Wallace hadn't budged. Grace flipped open her notebook, ran her finger down the list to spell number eight, "Make Andrew Wallace pee his pants in French," and marked it with a big *X*. She sighed, flipped the notebook closed as she exchanged looks with the others, and turned her attention back to the irregular verbs scrawled across the board at the front of the room.

When the bell finally rang, signaling the end of class, Jenny tightened the laces on her purple boots and carelessly pulled a loose thread out of one woolly sock.

"I'm disappointed," she said, shaking the thread from her fingers. "That would've been worth seeing."

"And he totally deserved it as well," said Adie.

"That time he pulled your chair out from under you, and you sprained your elbow. And that 'rat-tail hair' thing he said to Grace in front of everybody. What does that even mean, anyway?"

"It means," answered Grace, "that my hair's horrible and greasy and looks like rats' tails."

She tugged at a few dull, split-end strands. To others, she'd call her hair kind of sandy-colored, but it was more like mousy brown. And it never shone, no matter how much conditioner she used.

"That's so stupid," said Adie, pushing her own tightly curled dark locks out of her brown eyes. "I'd kill for your hair. You don't even have to use a flatiron. It's poker-straight all the time."

"I don't care what he says, anyway," said Grace. "Just thought he needed a short, sharp shock. How cool would it have been if it had actually worked?"

She looked up at Jenny, who was a little taller and the only athletic one in the bunch.

"How many spells is that now?" Jenny asked.

"Eight," said Grace.

"Well," sighed Adie, "ninth one's a charm. Wait and see."

"I won't hold my breath," Grace said, fixing her uniform tie so it sat neatly into her pressed collar. She slipped her schoolbag onto her shoulder and followed the other two out into the hallway. Halfway down the corridor, she felt the heavy weight of a body landing on her from behind.

"Ow! Knock it off, Una! You caught my hair!"

"Which is *not* rat-taily," Adie said quickly, catching Grace's bag as it dropped to the ground.

Grace shrugged her friend off her back and sighed as Una threw her arms around the other two. Her short, black bob framed her pretty elfin features as she gazed up at them eagerly.

"So did it work?" she said. "Did Andrew Wallace get his just reward?" Her gray eyes were lit up with excitement.

"Nope," said Jenny.

"Aw, fudge," said Una, slumping between them and sliding her arms from their shoulders. She shook her head and gave a very loud and exaggerated sigh.

"Had my fingers and toes crossed all the way through Spanish and everything. Why didn't it work?!"

"Maybe you have to use a more personal object," offered Jenny. "I mean something that the person really cares about. I'm pretty sure Andrew's not missing his math notebook right now."

"Come to think of it," said Grace, "I'm not sure I've ever seen him open that notebook."

"Oh God! Don't look now!" hissed Adie. "*The Beast.*"

The Beast was Tracy Murphy. Five foot ten inches of pure evil. Tracy wasn't overweight, but her solid mass was at least triple the width of any other girl at Saint John's. It was as if a professional football player had been packed into a schoolgirl's body, bulging with rippling muscle that threatened to burst at the seams. The intimidating look was topped off with dark red curls slicked back into a high ponytail and a thick layer of blue eyeliner beneath each dark, soulless eye. Tracy was the stuff of nightmares—and Una was her victim of choice.

"Hey, freak," Tracy snapped, giving Una's elbow a sharp dig, "I told you you're not allowed in this block."

Una's mouth opened and closed like a goldfish—but no sound came out.

"Leave her alone," said Jenny. With occult symbols and names of heavy metal bands Wite-Outed all over her schoolbag, Jenny looked a little tougher than the other girls. But though she was tall and always stood her ground, when it came to sheer size, she couldn't compete with the Beast.

"You'll be left alone," said Tracy, not taking her eyes off Una, "when you get out of my block. The D block's mine, and I don't like looking at your ugly *face*. So take it somewhere else."

"Yeah," a voice behind them snickered, "we don't like looking at your ugly face."

Grace glanced back at Bev, the larger of Tracy's devoted henchmen, and fought the urge to comment on the girl's ridiculously oversprayed hairdo. But Bev was never without Trish, who stood nearby, sporting an equally comical hairstyle, and if she dared insult either of them, their boss would surely intervene.

"Our lunchroom's in this block," Adie squeaked, "so she has to come through here."

"Then you'd better get into your *lunchroom*," Tracy sneered, leaning menacingly toward Adie, "before I lose my temper."

"Come on," Una whispered, grabbing Adie's hand. The four girls hurried to the safety of the room, trying not to run as Trish's and Bev's wicked laughter filled the hallway. They piled into the room, slamming the door and pressing themselves against it.

"So," said a musical voice. "You ran into her then?"

Startled, they turned together to see Rachel sitting on a table, with her feet on a chair. She was gazing into a small compact mirror as she swept some powder across her porcelain cheeks. Her pale blue eyes were already perfectly lined with black pencil, and her lips glistened with pink gloss. Glancing up, she snapped the compact shut and swung her legs onto the floor. Grace felt a pang of envy as Rachel's chestnut hair spilled over her shoulders in stylish, glossy layers.

"Yeah." Grace sighed and pulled her bag off her shoulders. "She's there every day now. It's getting worse."

"You okay?" Rachel asked, tipping her head toward Una.

"Yeah, I'm fine," Una mumbled, still blushing from the encounter.

"I don't get why she picks on you," said Rachel. "It's like she just chooses people at random."

"Just forget about it," said Una. "Let's talk about something else."

"Like a certain not-very-nice person peeing his pants in class?" said Rachel with a hopeful smile.

"Didn't work," said Grace, wiping the smile off her friend's face. "We think we're not picking personal enough items or something. Maybe we need his watch or his pen."

"Or his old gym shorts!" squealed Una.

"Ugh, gross!"

"Speaking of gross, are you *really* putting M&Ms on that sandwich?" Rachel looked in horror at Jenny, who was perched with her lunch box and a bag of candy on her knees.

"Honestly," said Jenny, "it's delicious."

"But there's coleslaw in there!"

"Trust me," Jenny said, gently sprinkling more M&Ms into her open sandwich, "my mom used to eat this all the time when she was pregnant with my little sister, and I thought it was the grossest thing ever. But then I tried it, and I swear I couldn't eat a sandwich without them now. Yum, yummedy-yum!"

The girls groaned in unison as Jenny took a great big bite and crunched loudly on the salad and sugar-coated chocolate mix.

"That'll do terrible things to your skin," said Rachel. She turned to Grace. "So more *personal* personal items then?"

"Maybe," said Grace, "but I'm just not sure we're going about this the right way. We've tried a bunch of spells, and not one of them has even slightly worked."

"What about that time we tried to get Mr. McQuaid to talk gobbledygook in history," said Adie, "and the next day he said 'French *Relovution*'?"

Grace raised an unconvinced eyebrow.

"I don't think that *was* us."

"It might have been us," Adie reasoned.

"If that was us," said Rachel, "it was pretty lame."

"Yeah," said Jenny with her mouth full. "What's the point of trying if *that's* all we can manage?"

"Ooh ooh ohh!" Una exclaimed suddenly. "I have the best idea. Let's do a love spell. That would be totally *awesome*."

"On whom?" asked Grace.

"What about James O'Connor?" said Rachel. "You like him."

"No, I don't!" cried Grace.

"Yes, you do. You blushed when he sat beside you in geography the other day."

"How would you know?" said Grace. "You were sitting *behind* me."

"Your ears went pink." Rachel grinned.

"Whatever," said Grace, her cheeks coloring. "I don't like him."

"Well, let's try it anyway," said Una, eyeing her

friend with a smile. "It probably won't work, so it doesn't really matter, does it?"

They all looked toward Grace.

"We can do it if you want," she said at last, sweeping her mousy brown hair out of her eyes and feigning a lack of interest. "I don't care."

"I'm taking that as a yes. Woo-hoo!" Una bounced to her feet, giving a little dancing wriggle. "This is gonna be so much fun."

"Will you sit down, Una?" Rachel said, cringing. "People can see in the window."

"Can't sit down," Una said, shaking her butt at Rachel as if she couldn't help it. "Too excited."

"Please knock it off, I'm begging you."

Una wriggled even more as a few students passing by outside pointed and laughed. Rachel hid her face in her hands.

"We're going to need something personal of James's," Jenny said.

"I'm in his English class after lunch." Una finally sat down, a little out of breath. "So I'll steal something out of his pencil case."

"Anyone else worried that people might start to notice we're stealing their stuff?" asked Adie.

"*Borrowing*," corrected Una. "*Borrowing* their stuff. And we'll give it back. You know, unless we can't or we forget."

✳✳✳

That Saturday night, at Rachel's house, the girls gathered together and watched eagerly as Jenny opened the huge leather-bound book on the floor. She flicked through the pages to the one marked "Love Spell."

"*The Great Book of the Occult*," she said grandly, as the others giggled and settled themselves in a circle on the carpet, "suggests the following procedure for 'awakening love in a reluctant other.'"

Jenny looked around and started to read.

"First, light one red candle and one white candle."

The candles were lit.

"Second, write the name of your intended love on a piece of parchment and repeat the following words:

Oh, Spirits, grant me love divine,
I wish his soul and heart be mine,
Though love, at first, may not be true,
Please make it so, I ask of you!

"Then there's an asterisk and this little note at the bottom of the page," Jenny said, turning the book so the others could read.

*Spells are performed at one's own risk. Neither the publisher nor the author is responsible for any injury/damage caused during the application of any procedures described in this publication.

The girls shrugged, then carried on chorusing the verse.

"Third and last," said Jenny, "dip the edge of the parchment into both flames and place in fire-proof container."

Grace watched the smoldering paper shrink in the

small bucket of sand until only a few charred pieces remained under a wisp of smoke.

"Well, that's that," said Jenny, closing the book with a snap.

"This one's going to work!" Adie's pretty olive complexion was glowing with excitement. "Grace, you'll probably have a love letter tucked into your locker door on Monday!"

"It's not going to work," said Grace. To hide her blushes, she picked up the bucket and tipped the sand into the wastepaper basket Rachel had taken from the bathroom. "And I don't care if it doesn't. Who wants to have someone sticking love letters in their locker? *So* embarrassing."

She was aware of all eyes on her as she left the room with the wastepaper basket's sandy remains. She hoped the fire in her cheeks would calm down by the time she returned to Rachel's room, but Adie's sympathetic smile told her it hadn't. She pretended to scratch her nose and flicked her hair over to hide her face.

"So what'll we do now?" said Una.

"I'm hungry," said Jenny. "Where did the snacks go?"

"We're saving them for a midnight feast," replied Rachel.

"And when will that be?"

"At *midnight*."

"And what time is it now?"

"Only ten thirty," Adie cut in.

"Are you joking?" Jenny said. "I'm not waiting 'til midnight."

She dove under a small pile of comforters, with Rachel right behind her. They struggled for a few giggling moments until Jenny emerged, victorious, with a packet of potato chips.

"And that's all you're getting!" Rachel said, swatting her with a pillow. "The rest is for later."

"Hey," said Una, "why don't we play Truth or Dare?"

"Ugh," replied Grace. "I hate that game."

"Ah, go on," said Una. "We'll each have a veto if there's a dare you really don't want to do."

"Does that work for truths as well?" asked Grace.

"We already know who you like," said Rachel, smiling, "so you won't need a veto on telling the truth."

Grace grabbed Jenny's bag of potato chips and fired it at Rachel. It bounced off her head.

"Ouch," Rachel said drily.

"I'll play," said Adie, "but no scary dares."

"Then what's the point?" cried Una.

"I'm with Adie there," said Rachel. "You always dare someone to go out to the Stone House, and there's *no way* I'm going out there in the dark."

The Stone House was a crumbling, ruined cottage at the end of the field next to Rachel's house. During the day, it looked lonely and broken, but at night, from the window of Rachel's bedroom, it became something sinister. The gaping roof revealed an emptiness so thick, it didn't look empty at all, and the jagged walls were like teeth, filling a dark mouth that was ready to suck in anyone who came too close…

"I don't *always* dare someone to go out there," argued Una. "But if I do, it's 'cause no one will do it."

"All right then," said Grace. "I dare you to walk out and touch the Stone House right now."

"We haven't started playing yet," Una said.

"Go on!" said Rachel. "If you do it, we all promise to play with no vetoes at all."

"Swear?" said Una.

"Yeah, swear," said Grace. "But you can't just walk near it and then run back. You have to stand right outside the door for at least a minute."

Una's brow furrowed, and Rachel smiled at her.

"Scared?"

"No," Una said. Getting to her feet, she pulled on her sneakers and grabbed her jacket.

"Don't let my parents see you go out!" Rachel whispered loudly as Una slipped downstairs.

The girls ran to the window and watched the bright pink jacket slowly make its way down the garden to the fence that surrounded the neighboring field. At the very end of the field, they could just make out the silhouette of the Stone House. They saw Una pause at the fence, then, in one quick,

17

decisive motion, grab it with both hands and flip her legs over to the other side.

Everyone was silent, watching the pink jacket gradually darken as Una left the comforting light of Rachel's house behind. Grace began to feel a little queasy and wondered if it had been a good idea to goad Una into this. One by one, the girls held their breath as the pale figure, barely visible in the dark, got closer and closer to the Stone House.

Suddenly, pale arms pumped through the dark, as Una came charging back toward the garden.

"I knew it!" said Rachel. "No one's ever done it."

Within moments, Una was back in the bedroom, peeling off her jacket and panting.

"You got close!" laughed Jenny.

"But not close enough," said Grace. "We keep our vetoes."

"I heard something!" said Una breathily. The girls laughed in reply.

"No, *seriously*," she said. "Like voices. There was someone there, I *swear!*"

Everyone laughed again.

"The only things out there making noise are the sheep," said Rachel.

"Whatever," said Una, sulking. "I know I heard something."

The others exchanged smiles but knew better than to tease her any further.

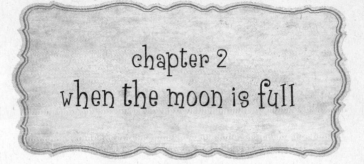

chapter 2
when the moon is full

Grace stamped through the school entrance, trying, in vain, to get Saturday night's love spell out of her mind. Would this be the one to work? Would James O'Connor be crazy about her this morning? A dull buzz from her phone broke her reverie. She fished it out of her pocket and opened the waiting text message.

OMG have best plan ever! Meet @ break

Grace frowned at Una's message, hoping it didn't involve anything risky or embarrassing. Una's plans usually did. Balancing her bag on one knee, Grace stuffed her heavy math textbook inside and slammed her locker door shut, too late to stop the small avalanche of notebooks that slid out. Grunting in dismay, she dropped her bag on the floor and began to pick up the fallen items.

"You missed one," a voice said. She looked up—and straight into James O'Connor's bright blue eyes.

"Thanks," she murmured, slowly taking the book he offered. Then she realized he was leaning in, and, for one heart-stopping second, she braced herself for the kiss that seemed inevitable—before exhaling quietly as he leaned past her to pick up his own bag.

Grace tried to flash him a quick, friendly smile as he left, but he was already chatting to his friends and didn't notice. She paused momentarily, then slammed the locker door shut with unnecessary force. *Of course it didn't work!* she said to herself.

✳✳✳

On their break, the girls all sat on and around the desks of the classroom, waiting patiently as Una looked ready to burst with her amazing plan.

"Right!" she squealed. "Are you ready for this?"

"Just tell us," sighed Rachel.

"Well, you know there's a Career Night in school on Wednesday?"

"Yeah," said Grace.

"We're going," said Una.

"Why?" asked Adie. "Seventh graders don't have to go, and it sounds really boring. It'll just be a bunch of people trying to get us to join the army or get into real estate."

"We're not going for the career advice," said Una, grinning. "We're going so we can sneak off to the P block."

"To do what?" said Rachel.

"Some Ouija boarding!"

"Ugh," said Adie. "We've done that loads of times, and it never works. The coin only moves when we all get tired and start leaning on it."

"But this time we'll be doing it *at school* and *at night*. How cool is that?!"

"Hold on," said Jenny, whipping her bag off the floor and tipping the contents onto one of the school desks. She grabbed a small, black book among the debris and flicked through it. "Yep, thought so. This Wednesday's a full moon."

"Perfect!" said Una.

"I don't know," said Grace. "What if we get caught? We'd be in *so* much trouble."

"Who's going to catch us?" said Una. "The teachers will all be distracted by the career stuff. All we have to do is wait 'til no one's looking and sneak off."

"What if we got locked in there or something?" Grace wasn't excited about this idea at all.

"I think we should do it," Rachel said suddenly with a grin.

"Yay!" Una exclaimed, clapping her hands with glee.

"And I've got the perfect surprise for it too."

"What?" asked Grace.

"You'll have to wait until Wednesday," Rachel said, still grinning.

***

The Saint John's Career Night was surprisingly busy and, Grace had to admit, surprisingly entertaining. By the time Una and Jenny arrived, Grace, Adie, and Rachel had already taken turns sitting on a police officer's motorcycle, talked in serious tones to an army representative about the pros and cons of living in barracks, and convinced a statuesque businesswoman that they were all determined to become models.

"Did you see her face," snorted Grace, "when she was saying how modeling requires good hair and good skin, and I was nodding away, scratching at this pimple on my chin?"

All three burst out laughing.

"I saw that," giggled Adie, "that's why I pulled out my hair band. Didn't even use conditioner in my hair this morning. She went white when she saw my impression of a Frizz Monster!"

"It's a good thing I was there," Rachel said with mock seriousness, penciling a little eyeliner on as she focused on her reflection in a nearby window. "She said I had the *perfect* complexion for modeling."

"*Whatever*," said Grace. "I think you've got enough eyeliner on now."

"Want some?" Rachel asked with a knowing smile.

Grace had asked to borrow some of Rachel's makeup once before, pretending she wore it all the time. She didn't realize it took some skill to apply and ended up jabbing herself in the eye with a mascara brush.

"Hey, there they are," said Adie, as Una and Jenny jogged toward them.

"Are we all set?" asked Una, not waiting for an answer. "We can slip away now, no bother. I haven't even seen a teacher yet. They're all inside the classrooms."

Taking one more sweeping look up and down the hall, the girls bundled toward the double doors that led to the P block.

Inside the block, the corridor was dark. None of the lights were on, and the only illumination came from the full moon that shone through the small, square windows. Their pace slowed, and they moved closer together as they suddenly felt very detached from the rest of the people in the building. The heavy doors muted the noise of the Career Night, and the girls felt like they were totally on their own. For some reason, they found themselves whispering.

They continued slowly down the shadowy hall until they finally reached the small, open area at the end.

"I have the board ready," said Una, kneeling down to unfold a large piece of paper. "Who's got a quarter?"

"No need," said Rachel. She sat down on the ground to open her knapsack and pulled out a box that looked like a board game. Smiling at the others, she opened it and pulled out a real Ouija board, like the ones they had seen on TV.

"Where did you get that?" asked Grace, grinning.

"Online," Rachel replied. "My sister bought it for me."

"Awesome!" gasped Una. "This just gets better and better. It'll definitely work now. Do you have the pointer thing too?"

"It's called a planchette," said Rachel, placing the pointer in the center of the board. There was silence for a minute as the girls took in the spooky sight of a real Ouija board bathed in moonlight. Then slowly they all sat down in a circle around it. Adie looked suddenly uncertain, but she sat quietly with the others.

"I'll take down anything the spirits spell out," said Grace, laying her notebook and a pencil on the floor beside her.

"You remembered your notebook—good job!" Una said. "Right. Everyone place two fingers on the…pancetta."

"*Planchette*," corrected Rachel.

The girls obeyed and took deep breaths as Una began to speak.

"If there is anyone there, please move the pointer."

Silence. She tried again.

"If there are any spirits with us, please move the pointer."

A little snort escaped Jenny's nose.

"Hey!" Una hissed.

"Sorry," Jenny said, suppressing a hysterical giggle. "The spirit stuff always gets me."

"This isn't going to work if you start laughing," chided Grace.

"I'll be good, I promise." Jenny wriggled from side to side, resettling herself to show she was now taking this seriously. Una closed her eyes and tried again.

"If there's anyone there, please move the pointer."

A sudden cool breeze swept over them.

"Did you feel that?" Rachel whispered.

"Shh!" said Una, her eyes snapping open as the planchette moved. The girls all froze as their hands rose ever so slightly with the pointer as it began to slide around the board.

"Who's pushing that?" Adie said, her voice barely a whisper.

"Not me," said Jenny.

"It's not me," Rachel said.

"Hush!" said Grace. "Watch it."

The planchette swung over the letter *t*, then *u*, the force beneath it getting stronger and stronger until the girls barely needed to touch it at all.

"I don't like this." Adie was close to tears. "I want to stop."

"Don't take your hand off," Grace said, her eyes glued to the pointer.

"I mean it," Adie continued. "I don't like this. It's too weird."

"But it's working!"

The pointer flew from letter to letter: *a, o, m, n, i, s.*

Adie snatched her hand away, holding it to her mouth in fear. The pointer didn't stop.

V, o, l, u, n, t, a, s.

Suddenly, Adie swept her hand over the board, sending the planchette flying into the wall. The others gasped as it landed heavily on the floor.

"What did you do?!" snapped Grace, still keeping her voice low. "You're not supposed to stop in the middle like that."

"This isn't right," Adie cried, the tears flowing steadily now. "I'm scared!"

"You're always scared!" said Grace. "I should take this down." She reached for her notebook.

The sound of fluttering pages made them all jump. Grace gasped and stared, horrified, as her notebook pages started flipping back and forth of their own accord in a crackling flurry of paper.

"What's *happening*?" she said, leaning away from it as far as she could and turning to the others for help. A scratching sound made her look back, and she saw her pencil, standing upright in the air as if held by an invisible writer, scrawling out letters across the page. Grace's breath caught in her throat, and she struggled to contain a scream. The pencil finished its journey in one final swirl and dropped lifeless to the ground.

It was a full minute before anyone dared to move. Slowly, in terrified silence, the girls helped each other to their feet, keeping clear of the notebook.

"We have to get out of here," said Jenny.

"I want to go home," said Adie, sobbing gently.

"Pack up the board," Jenny instructed Rachel, "and make sure it's well hidden in your bag."

Rachel hurriedly folded the Ouija board and stuffed it into her bag. Then, using her sleeve, just to be on the safe side, she picked up the planchette and threw it in on top of the board.

"The notebook," Jenny said urgently as the girls were about to head toward the exit.

"I don't want it," Grace said. "I don't want to pick it up."

"You have to," Jenny urged. "Someone will find it. It's got all our stuff in there. We can't leave it."

Grace looked at the white notebook lying in a square of moonlight, with the pencil lying half on and half off it. She walked reluctantly forward and kicked the pencil into the corner, then snatched up the notebook as if it were a hot coal and jammed it into her bag as quickly as possible.

"Let's go," Jenny said, herding them all toward the heavy double doors.

✳✳✳

No one said a word as they waited in the cool night air for their individual rides home. Adie had rubbed her face clean as best she could so her mother wouldn't see she had been crying. Grace kept a hand over her bag, convinced she could feel the notebook burning a hole through it. As the first of the parents arrived, she looked quickly at the others.

"Is everyone okay?" she asked. "I mean, as okay as we can be?"

"Yeah," replied Jenny. "As okay as we can be, I guess."

Rachel didn't answer but nodded slowly. Adie glanced up and frowned, then nodded too.

"Una?"

Una raised her head, then slowly turned to look at Grace with a strange half smile.

"Una?" Grace asked again. "Are you okay?"

"I'm fine, Grace. Thank you."

Grace frowned, and the others looked at Una, equally confused.

"Una?" Jenny said.

Una gave Jenny the same weird smile.

"Are you okay?" Jenny stammered.

"I'm fine, Jenny. Thank you," said Una in a mono-tone. The others stared at Una, and Grace could feel a knot gather in the pit of her stomach.

"Grace!" her mom called from the car. "Are you ready to go? Adie, you're getting a ride with us, aren't you?"

Nobody answered. All eyes were still on Una.

"*Grace*, are you coming?" her mom called again.

"Yes, Mom," Grace croaked, taking hold of Adie's sleeve with both hands and leading her toward the car. She couldn't help but look back at the strange sight behind them—Rachel and Jenny standing close together, a few feet from a perfectly serene, unblinking Una. She watched them as long as she could before the car pulled out of the school parking lot and the wall obstructed her view. She could sense Adie's anxiety behind her, but she didn't dare look back in case she dissolved into terrified tears herself.

"So how did it go?" Grace's mom asked.

"Fine," replied Grace.

"Fine? So you've all picked out your careers then?" her mom said with a wink.

"Yes." Grace wasn't listening. She was staring at the full moon, white and glowing in the dark sky above them, and feeling cold fear wash over her.

chapter 3
una's oddness

Thursday morning brought a fresh twist in Grace's stomach. She had eventually fallen asleep after hours of fretful tossing and turning, and had awoken to the horrible blaring of her alarm clock. For a brief moment, the events of the previous evening seemed nothing more than the echo of a terrible nightmare. But within seconds, the reality of it came flooding back.

Grace stepped over the threshold of the school entrance, hugging her bag to her chest like a life jacket. She was wondering whether she should go looking for the others when she saw Rachel, Jenny, and Adie standing nervously by her locker.

"You're here," said Adie, "thank goodness."

"How're you guys doing?" said Grace.

"Not good," replied Rachel. "I couldn't sleep a wink. Just kept tossing and turning."

"And anytime I did sleep, I was having nightmares," said Jenny, rubbing her eyes.

"Have any of you seen Una?" asked Grace. The others glanced at each other with troubled looks.

"I did," said Jenny.

"And?"

"She smiled and said, 'Hello, Jenny. Nice morning, isn't it?'"

Grace bit her lip and took a deep breath.

"Do you still have the notebook?" Jenny asked.

"Yeah," said Grace, "I didn't take it out of my bag."

"We'd better take a look at it, see what it says. I was going over the letters spelled out on the Ouija board last night, but they don't make any sense. They're just totally random."

Grace reached into her bag, bracing herself for heat or pain or something else. Feeling nothing but the cool pages of her notebook, she pulled it out and gave it to her friend. Jenny turned the pages of the notebook slowly, gulping as she silently read the penciled scrawl.

"Well?" said Adie. "What does it say?"

"Nothing," said Jenny, looking up.

"*Nothing?*"

"Well, not *nothing*. I mean there are words, but they're in another language or something."

Rachel snatched the notebook and read out loud, "*Tua omnis voluntas et ordinem.* Is that Italian, do you think? It's not Spanish anyway, or German."

"Or French," said Adie.

"Maybe Latin?" offered Grace. "It looks like that stuff we had to sing at church, Adie, remember?"

"Yeah, maybe it is Latin," Adie replied.

"We can translate it online then, if we know what language it is," said Jenny.

"I'm in computer studies this morning," said Rachel. "I'll check it out."

"Good," said Grace. "In the meantime, we need to keep an eye on Una. Either she's just totally freaked out about this whole thing or…"

No one wanted to say what the "or" might be. They nodded good-bye to each other and headed off to class.

✳✳✳

During their break, the four girls sat together on the floor in one corner of the A block. Rachel handed the notebook back to Grace.

"Your wish is my command," she said.

"Your wish is my command?" said Grace.

"Yeah," said Rachel, "I checked it out on a few different translation pages, and they all said pretty much the same thing."

"Your wish is my command," Grace repeated. "But we didn't wish for anything. What does it mean?"

"You got me."

Grace sighed and stared intently at the notebook, checking both the inexplicable Latin phrase and the old list of spells. Her own neatly written blue letters contrasted darkly with the scrawled pencil marks on the page. She held the book at the edges, noticing a small splash of what seemed like water near Andrew Wallace's name.

"Hello, girls."

They all jumped in unison and looked up to see Una staring down at them. Dropping her bag at her feet, she kneeled to sit next to them. Adie discreetly pulled her coat and bag close to her, so they wouldn't be touching Una's. There was silence as Una looked at each of them in turn, like she was analyzing their faces; all the while she wore that weird half smile. When she had taken in the whole group, she sat back on her heels, her neck long and her back straight, and folded her hands carefully in her lap.

"Hello, Una," said Grace, avoiding her friend's unnerving gaze. "How are you doing?"

"I'm fine, Grace. Thank you."

The horribly polite phrase filled them all with dread.

"You're okay after last night then?" Grace continued. "It scared us all a little."

"The Career Night?"

"Yes. And what happened after."

"The Career Night frightened you?" Una tilted her head, and a slight look of confusion framed her pretty face.

"The stuff in the P block did."

There was more silence as Una's hands slowly unfolded, slid over each other, and folded again. The rest of her body stayed perfectly still.

"It was dark in there without the lights on," she said finally, the eerie smile widening just a little. Adie hugged her coat for dear life.

"I guess so," said Grace.

The awkward silence descended again.

"Well, break's nearly over," said Grace. "And I have to get to my locker before class."

There was plenty of time left, but her heart was beating so hard, she thought everyone must be able to hear it. She had to get away from Una, fast.

"Adie," said Una, "we have English class now, don't we?"

The others watched Adie's face crumple.

"Yes, but I...yes."

"We don't want to be late," Una said, getting to her feet and waiting, completely still, as Adie picked up her things.

"No," Adie replied, flashing a look of helplessness at the others. She trailed down the corridor after their suddenly unrecognizable friend.

✳✳✳

Grace piled her books into her locker, barely caring as they slid in a mini-avalanche to the floor before she could shut the door. Slowly, she bent down to pick them up.

"You missed one," said a voice.

"Thanks," she said, snatching the offered book and firing it into the back of her locker.

"No problem," said the voice. "No problem at all. You look great today."

She started, whipping around to see James O'Connor's blue eyes gazing back at her.

"I, um…thanks."

"You always look great."

Grace glanced quickly around the block, wondering what was going on. Worried that this was some sort of setup, she slammed her locker door shut.

"I have to get to class," she said over her shoulder as she hurried away.

She ran all the way to her English class and was out of breath when she got there. Seeing that Jenny and Rachel were already sitting together, she took a seat at the table in front of them.

"God, I don't envy Adie right now," said Jenny. "Did you see the look on her face? What *is* wrong with Una? It's like she's *broken* or something."

"Maybe she's just in shock," suggested Rachel.

"Does that mean it'll wear off when she calms down?"

"I don't know."

"I'm not sure it's just shock," said Grace. "I mean, shouldn't it have worn off by now? Maybe Jenny's right. Maybe she's had some sort of breakdown."

"We should never have done that stupid Ouija board. We've scared her senseless!" said Jenny.

"Isn't it a little weird that Una's the one who freaked out?" said Rachel. "I mean, she's the one who's always up for this sort of stuff. In fact, *she* suggested it!"

"Yeah," Jenny agreed, "I would've thought if any of us lost it, it would be Adie."

Grace twisted around to lean toward the girls.

"Well, whatever the reason, Una is in trouble," she said, "and we have to figure out what we're going to do about it. I mean—"

"Mind if I sit here?"

The sudden presence of James and his piercing blue eyes gave Grace such a fright she squealed and toppled backward off the chair. Giggling erupted all around her as she struggled to right herself, ignoring James's proffered arm.

"Are you all right?" Jenny asked.

"I'm sorry," said James, who was now seated beside her. "I didn't mean to scare you. Are you okay?"

"I'm fine," replied Grace, turning to face the

whiteboard. She was in a daze. Mrs. Hennelly marched in without addressing the class and immediately began scrawling on the board. Feeling oddly detached from her surroundings, Grace took out her pen and copied down the notes. She didn't look at James until a few minutes into the lesson, when he nudged her arm and pushed his notebook toward her so she could read it.

James ♥s Grace 4EVER. A sudden sensation of pins and needles shot down Grace's legs and up her spine, forcing her to her feet.

"Aargh!" she exclaimed. More snickering laughter.

"I don't feel well, Miss!" said Grace. "I have to go to the bathroom." The laughter spread throughout the class.

"Quiet, everyone!" ordered Mrs. Hennelly with immediate effect. "Go ahead, Grace. But tell the school secretary to call home for you. You shouldn't be here if you're feeling sick."

Grace didn't answer or pause to collect her things or look at her friends. She hurried out the door and headed for the nearest girls' bathroom, sinking down onto the cool tiled floor. She held her head in her hands and took long, slow breaths.

What on earth is going on?

✳✳✳

It was lunchtime, and the four girls were deep in discussion.

"So the love spell has worked," Rachel said over her sandwich. "A little late, maybe, but it's worked."

"But *why?*" asked Grace. "Why *that* one? Why *now?*"

"I don't have a clue."

"Maybe we've got it," said Adie.

"Got what?" said Grace.

"Whatever power or skill witches get. I mean, that spell worked, the Ouija board worked. Maybe we're… well, maybe we're witches now. Maybe we've just…*got it.*"

They all considered this for a moment.

"Then what about Una?" said Jenny. "If we all got *the power*, or whatever, what's happened to her?"

"What if her mind couldn't handle it?" Adie replied.

"What if she just wasn't strong enough and the power has warped her brain?"

"I don't *feel* powerful," said Grace.

"Me neither," said Rachel. "I don't think we've *got* anything."

"So how do we fix Una?" asked Jenny.

"And reverse that stupid love spell," nodded Grace.

"I thought you'd be happy that it worked," said Rachel.

"Nope," said Grace, dropping her uneaten ham sandwich back into her lunch box. "It's just too weird."

✳✳✳

For Grace the rest of the day was a horrible blur of avoiding both Una and, now, James. As she dragged her feet on the walk home, she couldn't decide which one was creeping her out the most. James's unashamed stares and smiles made her blush, and more than one of their fellow students had noticed and started pointing it out. He seemed to almost welcome the teasing, like it confirmed a bond between them. On the other hand, Una's formality and politeness, so hideously out of character, was somehow frightening. Now it was extending to teachers as well. Her hand shot up when she knew the answer to a question, and Adie said she even offered to help Mr. Kilroy collect all the books at the end of class.

Being so distracted by her troubles, Grace didn't notice the large shadow cross her path until it was too late.

"Hey, look," Tracy's grating voice sneered, "it's a friend of the Freak. Hey, friend, where's the Freak?"

Grace kept her head down, didn't answer, and stepped around Tracy.

"I asked you a question." Tracy's tone hardened, and she slapped Grace's bag so it slipped off her shoulder. Grace stayed silent but picked up the pace a little. Grabbing the strap of the bag sharply, Tracy pulled Grace toward her until they were almost nose to nose.

"You tell the Freak I'll be especially looking out for her tomorrow. And you'd be best keeping your distance after that, know what I mean?"

Tracy's henchmen giggled, barely visible behind Tracy's awesome mass. Grace shrugged her off, frowning but not daring to talk back. As she hurried home, she realized her friend was in more than one kind of trouble. What if the new Una didn't *know* about Tracy Murphy's intense dislike? And if she dared speak to Tracy the way she was speaking to everyone else, Tracy would assume she was being made fun of in front of everyone and *definitely* knock Una's block off.

Grace called the others as soon as she got into the house. They were going to need a game plan in place by the next day.

✳✳✳

The plan next morning consisted of one very simple rule—keep Una as far away from Tracy Murphy as possible. Unfortunately, this meant that the girls could never leave Una alone, so they took shifts throughout the day depending on their schedules. Adie didn't want to take the first shift, but she was in both of Una's classes that morning, so it was the most practical. During the break, the girls herded Una out of the main building and behind the tennis courts, where they kept an eye out for the Beast and her cronies. Jenny had the next class, and Grace after that. Lunchtime was going to be the big problem. No one was allowed to leave the premises during lunch, so they had to stick to the school grounds. Their lunchroom was in Tracy's block, so that was definitely out. After much arguing back and forth, they agreed to sneak into one of the science labs and hide there at lunchtime for the time being.

"What a very well-equipped lab," said Una, gazing around.

Slowly chewing on their sandwiches, the girls tried their best to ignore Una's odd conversation.

"The gas taps on each desk are well-placed and, I'm sure, very useful," she went on.

Jenny let her head fall heavily onto her lunch box, knocking over the obligatory bag of M&Ms that scattered across the desk and onto the floor.

"You've made a mess, Jenny," said Una.

"Be quiet, Una!" Grace snapped, unable to contain herself any longer. But Una merely got up and wandered, humming, over to the window.

"When are we going to fix her?" Jenny grumbled, with her head still down on the desk.

"Tell me how, and I'll do it!" Grace replied.

"What if this is permanent?" Jenny said, finally lifting her head. "Do you think…?" She glanced at Una and lowered her voice. "Is she still *in* there?"

Grace looked up at Una's blank face staring at them and felt suddenly sad.

"She has to be," she said. "And we have to fix her soon. I've got a horrible feeling that the longer she stays like this, the worse it's going to get."

"Not to mention the fact that we're not going to be able to hide her from Tracy forever," said Adie.

"I think we need to go back to the Ouija board," Rachel said.

"What?" exclaimed Adie. "No. No way. I'm not

doing that again. That's what did this to her in the first place."

"It might be the only way to help her."

"What do you mean?" said Grace.

Rachel leaned forward and whispered, "What if she's *possessed?*"

Grace had considered the possibility but had been too afraid to say it out loud. She figured the others had felt the same.

"I don't know, Rach," she said, shaking her head. "It doesn't look like it does in the movies. I mean, she's not tearing anyone's head off or making objects fly around the room. She's just...well, *not herself.*"

"I think we should try going back to the board anyway," said Rachel. "It could be a quick fix."

"And what if it's not?" Adie asked. "What if it just does this to another one of us?"

"I'm not sure the board is the way to go," said Jenny. "We could try a spell, to make her normal again. I'm sure *The Great Book of the Occult* has something like that we can try."

"And what if *that* goes wrong?" said Adie. "If our spells are actually working now, we might do something terrible to Una if we don't get it right."

"Adie's right," Grace said solemnly, looking around at the others. "We just don't have a clue what we're doing."

✳✳✳

Grace, Adie, and Jenny sat quietly in Ms. Lemon's French class that afternoon. The realization that they had no idea how to help Una had left them all feeling utterly defeated. They gazed vacantly at the incomprehensible phrases that Ms. Lemon's marker scribbled across the whiteboard.

Grace was racking her brains for someone who could help them. They could search online, but the Internet was full of lunatics who probably didn't know any more than *they* did, but would try and charge them a fortune for nothing. They could tell their parents or a teacher, but who would believe them? And if they pointed out Una's strange behavior, some doctor would probably prescribe lots of pills and time in a psych ward in a hospital. No, they couldn't risk that. They would have to deal with this themselves.

"Ahh, gross!" Sally Martin jumped out of her seat and pressed against the next table, staring in disgust at the boy who had sat beside her. "The smell! Miss!"

Everyone leaned up in their seats or stood up altogether, trying to get a good look at Andrew Wallace, who was now fumbling with his bag and blushing so fiercely it looked like his head might burst. Ms. Lemon stepped forward to see what the matter was, and stepped back again quickly, looking very confused.

"Andrew, how did…" she stammered. "Are you all right? Why didn't you ask to go to the bathroom?"

"I…I don't know, Miss."

Andrew stood up, crouched over, trying to hide the evidence from the rest of the class. A sudden titter of laughter started at the tables nearest to him and gradually spread around the room.

"He peed himself!" a hissing whisper echoed around the class.

"That's enough, everyone!" Ms. Lemon shouted, trying to gain control of the rapidly growing hysteria. "Andrew, you're excused. I said *that's enough*! Everybody sit down and take out your textbooks!"

Grace, Adie, and Jenny were the only three to remain seated. Adie's and Jenny's faces had turned totally white. Grace's was bright red. She was blushing not out of embarrassment but out of complete shame. She remembered thinking how funny it would be for her old enemy, Andrew Wallace, to wet himself and run out of the classroom in mortification. But as she watched him escape through the door, clutching his bag to his front, she saw tears in his eyes, and it wasn't funny. It wasn't funny at all.

chapter 4
avenger's remorse

Another sleepover was arranged for that Saturday night, this time in Jenny's house. But no junk food or DVDs were brought along, and Una hadn't been invited. One by one, the four girls climbed silently up the ladder to Jenny's attic bedroom, settling in a circle on the floor, where Grace placed the open notebook.

Tua omnis voluntas et ordinem. Your wish is my command.

They all stared at the words scrawled below Grace's neat blue handwriting. Her orderly script listed all the spells they had tried since beginning their adventure in witchcraft.

"Of all the pages it could have written on," said Jenny, "it wrote on that one."

"It can't have been an accident," said Adie. "The pages were fluttering back and forth, all of them. It landed on that one because it was *looking* for that one."

"Now it's making that list of spells happen," Rachel said, pulling Jenny's bedspread around her shoulders.

"Why did we think that spell on Andrew would be funny?" Grace said quietly.

"I know," replied Jenny. "Did you see his face? That was awful. He'll never live that down."

"It was so mean," Adie agreed.

"So how long is this going to go on for?" asked Rachel. "I mean, are *all* the spells going to happen? And what then? Will Una go back to normal?"

Shielding Una from Tracy was exhausting, and the girls were glad for the break from her odd conversation and unblinking stares. Besides, they figured she was perfectly safe at home for the weekend. Unless, of course, her family had her certified for saying *please* and *thank you* all the time.

"I don't know," replied Grace. "If it's done the most

recent spell first, maybe it's working backward—the love spell, and then the pee spell—what's next?"

She twisted the notebook around to read it instead of waiting for an answer.

"Snow. It's the snow spell next."

"Well, that's not so bad," said Rachel. "What then?"

Grace froze, staring at the page, and her chin began to tremble.

"What is it? What's the next spell?" asked Adie.

"It's not the next spell I'm worried about," Grace whispered after a long pause. "It's what's at the *top* of the list—the very *first* spell we tried."

She picked up the notebook and held it out for someone to take.

"The first spell," she said, her hand shaking. "Our first spell."

Nobody took the notebook. They didn't need to read it. They all remembered what the first spell was.

"But we didn't mean that," cried Jenny. "Una was angry. She didn't mean it. *We didn't mean it!*"

"Does it count?" Rachel asked, beginning to panic.

"I mean, we'd only started. We didn't really know how to cast spells then. It was just a…it was just a trial. We didn't mean for it to work!"

"We followed the instructions in the book," Grace said. "It was done just like all the others."

She laid the notebook back on the floor, and all eyes went reluctantly to the top of the page.

Spell number one: Make Tracy Murphy get hit by a bus.

***

Later that night, Grace turned over in her sleeping bag and let her mind drift back to how it all started.

It had been just over two months before, when Jenny had arrived at Rachel's house with a black eye. Witchcraft was a brand-new idea to the girls, and they were having a meeting to cast their first spell. Jenny had brought the enormous leather-bound spell book, as promised, but all Grace could see was the shiny welt on Jenny's face.

"Oh my God!" she said. "What happened to you?"

"The Beast," Jenny replied.

"You're kidding," said Rachel. "Why did she go after *you*?"

"I was walking home with Una, and Tracy told her to hand over the bracelet she was wearing. The one Adie gave her for her birthday. I told her to get lost." Jenny gently scratched the swollen purple bruise around her eye. "She grabbed Una's arm, and I pushed her off. Then she punched me in the face."

"I can't believe it," said Adie. "What did your parents say? Did you tell them who did it?"

"No," said Jenny, "and they're really mad about it. But if my parents contact the school, it'll only make things worse. Tracy would get in trouble about it, and Una's life wouldn't be worth living."

Una arrived moments later, apparently even more upset than Jenny.

"Tracy just *hit* her!" she squealed. "Right in the face! It was so horrible. I'm so sorry, Jenny. This is all my fault. I just wish there was something I could do about it."

"Don't be silly. It's not your fault," Jenny replied.

"Hey," said Rachel, "I was thinking, if we're going to try out something from *The Great Book of the Occult* tonight, why don't we cast a spell on the Beast? Like a revenge spell or something?"

"Yeah!" said Grace. "That's perfect. Something we all really want. Maybe that'll help it to work."

"Definitely," said Una, her voice low and determined. "I definitely want to try that."

When everything was arranged according to the book's instructions, the girls sat in a circle around a lit candle and a piece of card adorned with Jenny's crudely drawn pentagram. Una tossed Tracy's compass onto the floor, next to the candle. Tracy had once used the compass to try and poke her in the back, but had missed and left it lodged in Una's bag strap instead.

"Right," said Grace, "I'll say the spell, and you all hold hands and concentrate on the candle's flame. Remember, don't break the circle 'til I've blown the candle out."

She settled herself on her haunches, took Rachel's hand to her right and Adie's to her left, and took a deep breath.

"O, Guardians of Vengeance sweet,
Give hope and power and peace to us,
Allow dark magic's awesome feat—"

"Make Tracy Murphy get hit by a bus!"

Taken aback by Una's sudden interruption, Grace was too slow to stop her before she leaned forward and, with one sharp breath, blew out the candle.

"Una!" she cried. "That's not the verse we wrote!"

"It's the one we should have written," Una said, frowning as she dropped Rachel's and Jenny's hands.

"But what if it works?" said Grace.

"What if it does?" replied Una. "She deserves it."

She looked around at the uncertain faces of her friends.

"*Relax*, it's not going to work," she said, after a pause. "I'm bored with all this magic stuff. Let's watch a movie."

"No action movies, please," pleaded Adie.

"And I'm not watching a chick flick," said Grace.

Rachel took Adie and Una downstairs to riffle through the DVD collection in the living room, while Grace and Jenny cleared up the remains of their first venture into magic.

"You don't think it'll really work, do you?" said Jenny.

"I don't know," said Grace. "No, not really. Still…"

"She probably does deserve it," said Jenny, gently rubbing her eye again and wincing as she neared the sorest part. "Not just for this, I mean. But for all of it."

"Yeah." Grace nodded. "She probably does deserve it. I just wouldn't want to be the person who does that to someone else, you know?"

"Yeah, me neither."

✳✳✳

After the realization that their spells had started working—and the shocking reminder of the nature of their first one—the girls had lain awake almost all of Saturday night imagining the moment when Tracy Murphy would meet her maker. On Sunday morning, they got up, one by one, filled with dread. Subdued, they parted company, and each spent the day looking out of the windows of her own home and fearing the worst.

Although Monday morning dawned bright and sunny, in math class Rachel nudged Grace and nodded at the classroom window. Grace looked up and watched, horrified, as the first gentle flakes glided to the ground. In less than ten minutes, they had picked up furious speed, and by the time an emergency announcement had been made over the intercom instructing everyone to head home immediately, there was a full-on blizzard engulfing the school.

"It's bizarre," Grace heard the vice principal say to one of the teachers as they battled their way down the corridor through hordes of rushing students. "It's just this town. Nowhere else in the state. It's like we're stuck in a snow globe."

Outside, the school grounds had turned perfectly

white, and still the snow fell and the wind picked up. Land Rovers and other big cars arrived as those parents who could reach the school took away students. A few enthusiastic kids attempted to make snowmen and throw snowballs while they waited for a ride, but the ferocious weather worsened until everyone was forced back inside the main building. Grace and the others huddled by a radiator for warmth.

"My dad's truck might get through," said Jenny. "He could take you all home."

"Have you called him?" asked Adie.

"No signal," Grace cut in. "No one's getting any signal in this weather."

"We're all going to be stuck here," said Adie, "everyone who's left. It's just getting worse out there. Not even the four-by-fours can get through now, I bet."

Adie was right. By this time, no traffic could navigate through the wall of snow. The principal stood on the stage in the main hall and announced that, in all likelihood, they would all be there for the night. Groans and wails could be heard around the hall, and some crying from a few desperately unhappy and frightened students. The remaining teachers hurried in and out of storerooms and classrooms, trying to scrounge together blankets and food. The vending machines were opened and emptied, but not even a steady stream of chocolate and potato chips could lift spirits. The kids were cold and hungry. They wanted real dinners. They wanted to be safe and warm at home.

"At least Una got out," Jenny sighed, stealing some of Rachel's coat to cover her freezing knees. "Saw her dad pick her up when the cars could still get past the gates. Imagine being stuck here with her rambling on for hours."

"Are you all right, girls?" They all looked up to see Ms. Lemon's concerned face.

"Not really, no," groaned Adie.

"We're all right, Miss," Grace said. "But are we definitely stuck here all night?"

"I'm afraid it looks that way," replied Ms. Lemon.

"Even if they get the police out, or something, I can't see them making any headway…it's just too strange…"

Grace frowned as their French teacher seemed to drift off for a moment, staring into the middle distance like she was working out a puzzle.

"Anyway," she said, shaking her head quickly, "if you girls get too cold, or if you need anything, come and tell me."

"We will, Miss. Thanks," Grace replied.

The girls huddled closer together as she walked away.

"Anyone else feeling horribly guilty right now?" said Adie.

"Shh!" said Grace. "Keep it down."

"Oh, no one's listening," Adie sighed. "They're all too cold and hungry. And it's all our fault."

"All we asked for was *a little* snow," said Rachel sulkily. "How is this a little snow? We didn't ask for a blizzard. We just wanted to have a snowball fight."

"We asked for *real* snow," snapped Adie.

"Real snow for a snowball fight," said Rachel, raising her voice. "We just wanted to make sure it would stick. That it wouldn't just be sleet or something. We didn't ask to get snowed into *school!*"

"Stop it!" rasped Grace, trying to keep her voice to a whisper. "People can hear you. What does it matter what we asked for? This is what we got. We can't do anything about it now."

"Well, we're going to have to do something about it," Jenny said quietly. "Not just the snow, but all of it. This is what? Spell number seven? Not far to go to number one. And we still don't have a clue how to stop it."

That shut them all up.

"Hey, Grace." James O'Connor came hurrying across the main hall, his jacket held out to her and his voice way too loud. "Here, put this on. You must be freezing."

"Have my jacket, Grace. You must be *freeeezing!*" someone mimicked in the crowd. That was followed by some nasty giggling, which, luckily, didn't last long. After all, teasing is hungry work, and there was no hope of dinner.

"Aw." Adie obviously couldn't help herself. "That's really nice."

James beamed at her as he wrapped the jacket around Grace's shoulders. Grace shrugged it off and surreptitiously kneed Adie in the leg.

"I'm fine," she said. "My jacket's enough. You should keep your own, James. You'll get cold."

"Don't be silly. You have it."

He tried again to close it around her and, again, she shrugged it off. In the end, he made do with placing it clumsily over her feet, patting it gently as if it might slip off and expose her ankles to a deadly chill. Grace pretended not to notice and kept her head turned toward her friends in the hope that he would think them deep in conversation. But the girls offered no help, they just stared, round-eyed, from Grace to James and back again as if they were at a tennis match. Eventually James settled himself on the ground beside Grace, and the only way she could avoid his eyes was to close her own. The others sat silently, waiting to see what would happen next. But James's loving glances and Grace's lack of response soon grew tedious, and they each drifted off to sleep in the uncomfortable cold.

***

"Rise and shine, people! Time to get up!"

It was just after dawn and the principal's joyous voice rang out through the main hall. Half-asleep students began climbing to their feet.

"In another bizarre twist to the weather, the snow has cleared up completely. Your parents have started arriving outside. Everyone is excused from school today, teachers included. I think you all need a real rest at home after such a horrendous night. Thank you for your patience, and have a safe trip home."

The girls followed the stream of uniforms heading for the door, and Grace finally managed to lose James in the jostling crowd. The girls struggled to keep their eyes open. Their backs and necks were stiff from sitting or half-lying on the hard floor of the hall, and they rubbed their shoulders to try and ease the discomfort.

"Well, there's my dad," said Jenny. "Anyone need a ride home?"

"My mom's over there," Grace replied, pointing.

"Mine just texted," said Adie. "She's on her way."

"Mine too," said Rachel.

"Okay then." Jenny sighed. "I guess I'll see you all tomorrow."

"Yeah," said Grace, "see you, guys."

She dragged her feet as she made her way slowly to her mom's car. Patricia Brennan was already out of the car and hurrying toward her. She caught her daughter in a big bear hug.

"Are you all right, sweetheart?" she gasped, hugging her tightly. "I was so worried. We all were. Nobody's parents could get through. It was awful!"

She pulled Grace back so she could look at her.

"You look so tired, love. Are you okay?"

Grace's nose was stinging with the tears that

threatened to pour out, so she simply pursed her mouth in a tight smile and nodded vigorously.

"Oh, you poor thing!" her mother said, hugging her again.

Grace wished her mom would let go and get back into the car. She was afraid she would burst out crying in the middle of the school parking lot. She leaned back, indicating she was ready to leave, and they both got into the warm car, her mother occasionally glancing at her with a sympathetic smile.

Back at home, Grace's mom reheated a hearty stew and placed a big bowl of it in front of Grace. On a large blue plate she piled homemade muffins and scones.

"When did you make all this?" asked Grace.

"During the night. I was too worried to sleep," her mom said with a tired smile.

Grace bit back the tears again and began devouring the hot, tasty stew. Still hungry, she managed to finish off two muffins and half a scone with butter and jam. When her belly was full, her eyelids became suddenly heavy.

73

"Off to bed now, love," her mom said softly, almost lifting her off the chair and up the stairs. "You need to get some rest."

"I have to talk to the girls," Grace muttered, barely awake.

"Later, hon," her mom said, tucking her into bed.

"It can't wait," Grace continued to mumble. "Poor Una."

"Are you worried about Una?" her mom asked. "I didn't see her with you at the school. I can call her parents, if you want."

"They don't know," Grace's voice was barely audible. "They weren't there."

Her mom frowned for a moment, then decided her daughter was probably already half asleep and dreaming. She kissed her forehead and left, closing the door gently behind her.

chapter 5
a match for the beast

"Girls, give me a hand with this, would you?" Ms. Lemon called as Grace and Adie crossed the school parking lot.

They hurried over to help the teacher with the large suitcase she was trying to haul out of the boot of her car.

"It's really heavy, Miss," said Grace, struggling with the weight as they lowered the bag to the ground. "What's in it?"

"Oh, just some odds and ends," the woman replied. "You know, for class."

"For class?" said Adie.

"Hmm, well not *your* class. Another class."

"It smells funny, Miss," Adie said, turning up her

nose as a puff of dust flew up from the tattered-looking material.

"It's old, Adie," said Ms. Lemon. "It's been gathering dust for a few years, I'm afraid."

"Do you need help carrying it in, Miss?" asked Grace.

"No need, girls. See?" Ms. Lemon pulled up one end of the bag by the handle, and it began to roll along the ground on a pair of very squeaky wheels.

"Thanks, you two," she said. "You can run along now. Don't be late for class."

Obediently, they headed into the main building and toward Grace's locker, which had become their regular rendezvous point each morning. The other two arrived a few minutes later.

"Anything to report?" asked Grace.

"Only that my parents nearly lost it over the snow thing," replied Jenny. "You should have heard the stuff my dad was going to try to get to the school. He went halfway across the state to rent a tractor and trailer. He was going to try and fit all the stuck students on top of it! Luckily, my mom talked him out of it. I would've been mortified."

"At least we got a day off from school out of it," said Rachel.

"Wasn't worth it," said Grace.

"No way," said Adie. "My mom was nearly in hysterics about it. She's still worried I might have delayed frostbite or something. It'll be ages before she calms down."

The piercing sound of the school bell rang out loudly through the halls, followed by a low collective groan from all of them.

"Fudge," Jenny said, picking up her backpack. "I really don't feel like math this morning."

"Where's Una?" asked Grace suddenly.

"What?" said Jenny.

"Who's got Una this morning?"

"Adie," said Rachel.

"No," said Adie, frowning. "I don't have her 'til English. After the break. It was Grace's turn."

"No," said Grace, beginning to worry. "I don't have her 'til after lunch. Jenny?"

"She's in none of my classes today."

Grace looked from one to the other of her friends. "Then where *is* she?"

They stood on tiptoes to look over the crowd and down the corridors, but Una was nowhere to be seen.

"We have to go look for her," said Grace. "Jenny, you and Rachel head that way. Me and Adie will take the other side. Go all the way up, and we'll meet you at the opposite end of the building."

The girls spilt up and hurried toward the corridors that linked the large blocks of the school. As Grace and Adie passed the doorway that led out the gym, they heard the now-familiar monotone reply.

"I'm fine, Tracy. Thank you."

"Oh, God," said Adie, grabbing Grace's arm and pulling her through the open door.

Una stood surrounded by Tracy, Trish, and Bev. The Beast stood right in front of her, hunching over so they were nearly nose to nose. Una seemed completely unaware of the danger and replied to Tracy's snarl with her strange wide-eyed smile.

"I have to go now, or I'll be late for class. You should probably go too, Tracy."

"We're not going anywhere," Tracy growled, grabbing Una by the collar and pushing her back until they were out of sight of the doorway.

"You're hurting my neck," Una said calmly.

"Leave her alone!" Grace's voice was shaking.

Adie sheltered behind her friend, still holding on tight to her sleeve, and peeked her head over Grace's shoulder.

"Yeah!" she said, and ducked down again.

Tracy barely seemed to notice them. She twisted Una's collar in both hands, pushed her back against the wall, and lifted her clear off the ground.

"Put me down, please," Una said, her voice a little constricted.

"Ha, ha!" laughed Trish. "Did you hear her? *Put me down, please.* Ha, ha!"

"Put me down, please!" Bev echoed, and grinned at her friend.

Tracy leaned in, glaring at Una with her dark,

menacing eyes. She bunched one fist. Then suddenly her expression changed as she watched Una's eyes. They were turning red.

Una drove her knee upward until it connected sharply with Tracy's stomach, forcing the Beast to drop her. Then, with her face as passive as ever, Una swung her right arm and caught Tracy on the cheek with her fist, knocking her clean off her feet to the ground.

Grace and Adie stood shocked, frozen to the spot even as Jenny and Rachel ran into them from behind.

"What happened?" gasped Jenny. "Is Una okay?"

Grace tried to answer, but her voice caught in her throat. She couldn't take her eyes off Una as she made her way toward the girls, her bright red irises fading back to their usual gray.

"Her eyes," Rachel croaked. "Did you see…?"

Grace still couldn't speak. As her friends gripped her sweater, and each other, she desperately wanted to run as Una stopped in front of her, but her legs were too weak to move.

"Hello, girls," Una said pleasantly. "I'm afraid we're late for class."

Grace stared into the sweet gray eyes, hardly able to believe that just a few seconds ago they were burning bright red, like fire—they weren't her eyes. They belonged to someone else.

Her friend wasn't in shock. She hadn't had a nervous breakdown. Rachel was right—someone or *something* else was inside Una.

"What's going on here?" the vice principal's voice suddenly boomed.

Tracy's henchmen wasted no time.

"Sir!" yelled Bev. "Una punched Tracy in the face. For no reason, sir."

"Yeah, sir," followed Trish. "I saw it as well. Tracy wasn't doing anything, sir."

"All of you to my office. *Now!*" said Mr. Collins.

Trish and Bev helped the Beast to her feet and faked concern as she cradled her face in her hand and put on a slight limp. As they passed the *non*-Una, Tracy flashed her a look of pure hatred. This was not over.

"Sir," said Grace quietly. "It wasn't…*Una's* fault, sir."

"I said everyone to my office, Grace," said Mr. Collins. "And you can all explain yourselves there."

The chaos that ensued in Mr. Collins's office eventually required the summoning of parents to the school. Petrified that whatever had control of their friend would lose its temper once more, Grace and her friends tried to explain that Una had been bullied for weeks, while Trish and Bev described a nunlike Tracy set upon by a vicious girl for no reason at all. Mr. Collins, like all the teachers, was well aware of Tracy's reputation, but he could not ignore the enormous welt that had quickly appeared on Tracy's cheek. In the end, it was decided that both were at fault, and so both were to be suspended.

"This is outrageous!" Tracy's diminutive, but ferocious, mother shrieked. "My daughter gets punched in the face by this little delinquent, and she's sent *home*? You'll be hearing from my lawyer about this."

The Beast was easily a foot taller and wider than her mother, but she leaned against her like a wounded kitten. When Mr. Collins wasn't looking, she scowled at Grace.

"If you feel it necessary to contact your lawyer, Mrs. Murphy"—Mr. Collins sighed—"I can't do anything to stop you. But both girls are still suspended."

Mrs. Murphy left quickly with her daughter when she realized the vice principal was not to be dissuaded. Una's father seemed a little perplexed by the whole thing. His daughter had a penchant for getting herself into trouble, but certainly not the violent kind. Her recent calm, polite reaction to any situation just seemed to confuse him even further. He left the school in a little bit of a daze, with his perfectly serene daughter marching brightly behind him.

The girls were now free from babysitting Una for the rest of the week, but they would much rather have been saddled with her weird conversation than have witnessed that morning's events.

"That's it, then," said Rachel in their lunchroom. "We *have* to go back to the Ouija board."

"No!" Adie cried.

"No, no, no," said Jenny, shaking her head. "We need an exorcist or something. To drive the spirit out."

"If it does that to Tracy Murphy for holding it against a wall," Grace said gently, "what'll it do to us for trying to drive it out of Una's body altogether?"

"Exactly," said Rachel. "Whatever we're going to do, we have to do it fast. And before Una realizes what's happening. I don't want to be on the receiving end of that thing if this doesn't work."

"Her eyes were red," mumbled Adie.

"I know," replied Grace. "And her face was so…so *calm*. Like she was swatting a fly or something."

"Come on," said Jenny, getting impatient. "We need a plan. Does anyone have any ideas at all?"

"I vote we just tell our parents," said Adie firmly. "We don't have a clue what we're doing here."

"Neither will they." Grace frowned. "They won't believe this was any kind of magic. They'll just have her taken to the hospital or something. No, we need someone who knows magic. Someone who knows all about the supernatural."

"What about Old Cat Lady, Grace?" Rachel suddenly blurted out.

"Mrs. Quinlan?"

"Some kids at school say she's a witch!"

"She's not a witch," groaned Jenny. "She's just some old woman who's gone around the bend."

"How do we know that?" asked Rachel. "Maybe she *is* a witch."

"Who lives in a duplex in Wilton Place?" Adie sighed.

"Maybe," replied Rachel. "How do *we* know how a witch would live? I mean, she's got lots of cats."

"Oh, well, that confirms it then," said Grace.

"Hey, at least I'm trying."

"You're right, you're right. I'm sorry," soothed Grace. "I guess we could at least go talk to her. What do we have to lose?"

"Not a thing," said Jenny.

chapter 6
the witch in wilton place

Every town has at least one unfortunate resident who, because of age, infirmity, crankiness, loss of mental faculties, or all of the above, becomes known as the local crazy person. Mrs. Quinlan was one such person.

She lived in a neighborhood not far from the school grounds, in a run-down house teeming with cats, and kept very much to herself. Her frizzy gray hair and pale eyes made her moth-eaten, disheveled clothes look even older than they were, and her shrill voice and fierce looks scared any children who dared approach her.

The Saint John's schoolkids loved to tell terrible tales about her—that she cursed those who dared to call to her house, that in each flea-bitten cat was the captured soul of someone who had dared to cross her, and, courtesy of a particularly imaginative eleventh grader, that she had killed and eaten her own husband.

Obviously, there was no evidence to support any of these rumors, but they persisted. Parents hushed their sons and daughters when such stories were brought up at the dinner table, but then gently instructed them to keep clear of old Mrs. Quinlan.

On Thursday afternoon, when the final bell had rung for the day, the girls slowly crossed the football field, clambered through the wiry hedge behind the school, and out into the cul-de-sac of Wilton Place. Mrs. Quinlan's dilapidated house was the very last one. It looked dark and lonely, in sharp contrast to the other, much better kept, houses of the neighborhood. Already, the girls could see a couple of the infamous, soul-filled cats lazing in the front garden. The girls inched forward, none of them willing to be the first to reach the driveway.

"Hold on," said Grace, putting out her hands to halt their slow progress. "What are we going to say?"

"Ahem," Jenny mused, "what about, 'Hey, Old Cat Lady, we were wondering if you're a witch 'cause our friend's possessed by a spirit or something and soon we're going to kill the school bully. Got a spell for that?'"

Grace couldn't help but think, despite Jenny's sarcasm, that that was exactly what they *needed* to say. But somehow, they'd have to approach the subject with a little more subtlety.

"Why don't we say we're doing a school project or something?" suggested Rachel. "And ask for help."

"What kind of project?" asked Grace.

"I don't know...about the area. About Wilton Place. Yeah! We can say we're collecting stories from long-term residents about the history of Wilton Place. You know, and the school. Modern history and all that."

"Ancient history, more like," mumbled Jenny. "Have you seen Old Cat Lady?"

"Let's avoid calling her that for the moment," warned Grace. "Everyone be as polite as possible." She hitched her bag higher onto her shoulder. "Everyone ready? Let's go."

The girls huddled tightly together as they reached the front step, right in front of the door. Adie held on to Jenny's bag as she leaned backward, glancing right and left at the sleepy-looking cats, searching for human souls in their slow-blinking eyes.

"Right," said Grace, taking a deep breath, "here goes."

She linked Rachel's arm, just in case the others spooked and ran off at the first sounds of life within the house, then reached up to grasp the wreath-shaped knocker.

Bang, bang, bang.

They waited. Nothing happened.

Grace shrugged and tried again.

Bang, bang, bang.

They waited again.

"Maybe she's out," said Jenny.

"Yeah," said Adie, "I guess even crazy old ladies—*aaagh!*"

They all jumped to see a pair of pale eyes glaring

at them through the frosted glass beside the door. Suddenly, the door was wrenched open and Old Cat Lady stood before them in all her moth-eaten glory.

"*What do you want?!*" she shrieked, spittle flying from the corners of her mouth as she spoke.

"I—um—we—" Grace stammered. It was taking up all her energy not to turn and run. She gripped Rachel's arm with all her might. Rachel in turn was holding on to Adie, who held on to Jenny. Somehow they managed to stay rooted to the spot.

"Well?" More spittle. "I said, *what do you want?*"

"We're studying the history of the area," Rachel's confident voice suddenly chimed. "We're talking to local residents about their memories of Wilton Place and Saint John's School. It's part of our history curriculum—a small project on modern history. We were wondering if we could ask you a few questions."

Rachel beamed brightly, as if she'd surprised herself. Grace and the others exchanged impressed glances.

"History?" Mrs. Quinlan said, squinting at her. "I

don't know anything about history. Now clear off. All of you."

The girls were protesting when, suddenly, a small ginger kitten shot past Mrs. Quinlan's feet and out into the garden.

"Damn it!" the woman hissed. "Catch it, then! Don't just stand there! *Catch it!*"

Spreading out across the dry, brown lawn the girls ran about, tripping over themselves and each other, before Jenny managed to snatch the little creature by the scruff of the neck. She tucked it into the crook of her arm and stroked it gently as it hooked onto her school sweater with its little claws.

"Bring it here," said Mrs. Quinlan, flapping her hands in Jenny's direction. "It's not supposed to be out."

Jenny unhooked the kitten and placed it into the woman's outstretched hands. Mrs. Quinlan cradled the little animal, then looked at the girls suspiciously.

"What sort of questions are you asking? How many of them?"

"Oh, just a couple," Grace replied. "It won't take long. We promise."

Mrs. Quinlan snorted loudly, then turned to go back into the house.

"I suppose you can come in for a minute," she growled, as she disappeared inside. "Shut the door behind you."

The dark hall smelled funny. Like damp clothes and animal fur. As they passed doorways on the left side and stairs on the right, the girls could hear muted meows all around.

"She must have dozens of cats in here," whispered Adie. Then she tapped Jenny lightly on the elbow. "Hey, did you look into that kitten's eyes?"

"Yeah."

"And?" Adie pushed.

"And what?"

"Did you *see* something in its eyes?"

"Yeah," breathed Jenny.

Adie froze. Jenny smiled.

"Conjunctivitis."

Adie scowled and followed the others into the ramshackle kitchen at the end of the hall. The smell was even stronger in there. Cat beds and litter boxes lined the edges of the room. On the kitchen table, a wire cage housed a very sorry-looking animal. It hissed angrily at them, baring its yellowed teeth and arching its back, making its balding, patchy fur look even more unsightly.

"That cat looks a little mangy," Rachel said to the old woman. "What's wrong with it?"

"Mange."

"Oh. Well, shouldn't you let it out to get some exercise or something, so it can get better?"

"I can't let it out, you fruit loop," the woman snapped. "It'll infect the others. Have to keep it isolated while it's being medicated."

"How come you have so many cats?" asked Grace.

"Some are mine. Some are fostered. They go to new homes when they're socialized and healthy. Any more questions about general animal welfare, or are you going to get to the point?"

Given the woman's testy mood, it didn't seem like a good idea to launch into the witch question, so the girls asked a series of awkward and uninteresting questions about the history of their school and the surrounding area.

"Attended Saint John's myself," Mrs. Quinlan said, a little more relaxed now as she sat, gently stroking the orange kitten in her lap.

"It was built back then?" Jenny asked.

"Yes, it was built *back then*," the woman snapped. "I'm not that old, you know."

Looking at her this closely, Grace could see that Old Cat Lady was, in fact, not nearly as old as they presumed her to be. She could have been in her early fifties, or even late forties, though her sallow and weather-beaten face made her look that much older. It didn't help that she dressed like she'd just stepped out of a trash can.

"It was a different place then, of course." Mrs. Quinlan gazed at the ceiling. "None of these new technology things, PC computers and all the rest. We learned the good old-fashioned way—with black-boards and chalk."

"We have interactive whiteboards now," said Rachel.

"And the teachers didn't take any lip," the woman continued, ignoring the interruption. "The kids weren't rude like they are nowadays. If you caused any trouble, you were given a good beating. And you didn't cause trouble again."

She pursed her lips and gave them all a look.

"What happens nowadays, hmm?" she went on. "The parents are called, and the teachers and the students all talk about their *feelings*, and *why* the brat misbehaved. It's all that psycholosophy garbage now. Don't know how to raise kids anymore, that's the problem! Bring back the ruler, that's what I say."

She fell silent, still staring into the distance as if she could see the old schoolrooms right in front of her. Grace let this heartwarming sentence settle before going on with her questions.

"And what sort of hobbies did you have?"

"Hobbies? The usual, I suppose. Sports, though I wasn't much for that. I liked reading a lot."

"Really?" said Grace. "What sort of books? Mysteries, thrillers, horrors…the occult?"

"The what?" the woman snapped, narrowing her eyes at Grace.

"Oh, I was just wondering what sort of books you liked reading."

"I got that much, Einstein."

"Right, well…um…nowadays everyone our age is big into the supernatural stuff. You know—vampires, werewolves…witches. That sort of thing. Was that what you and your friends liked to read?"

"I read some books like that." Mrs. Quinlan was now scrutinizing Grace's rapidly reddening face with suspicion.

"That's cool," Grace replied, avoiding her gaze. "We like that stuff too. And about witches, in particular. And witchcraft. You know, spells and stuff."

"Uh-huh."

"And sometimes we think, wouldn't it be fun to, you know, *do* spells. And stuff."

"*Do* spells?" the woman said.

"Yeah. Did you ever think it might be fun to do spells?"

Mrs. Quinlan's brow furrowed as she sat in silence. Grace, feeling sweat break out at the back of her neck, raised her eyes to look directly at the woman in front of her.

"Did *you* ever do spells?" she said quietly.

Mrs. Quinlan paused, slowly stroking the sleeping kitten in her arms.

"Did *I* ever do spells?"

Grace looked helplessly at the woman and nodded slowly.

"What class was this for again?" Mrs. Quinlan looked at each of them calmly.

"It's not for a class," Grace said. "We need to ask if you're a…if you're a…a witch."

Mrs. Quinlan's eyebrows shot up toward her graying hair and her mouth went into a hard line.

"Well, my, my, my," she whispered. "I've had some

brats come to my door in the past, but none as sneaky as you all."

She stood up slowly, tipping the kitten onto the floor, and loomed over the girls, her eyes narrowed to slits. Her voice was low and menacing.

"Out you go, now," she said.

"Let's get out of here, Grace," Adie whispered urgently, tugging at her friend's sweater.

"Please, Mrs. Quinlan! We need help," Grace said. "We don't know who else to turn to."

"Out. Now." The woman's voice was still frighteningly quiet. She began to inch around the table toward them.

"*Now*, Grace!" Adie's voice became frantic. "Jenny? Rachel? She'll curse us. She'll…"

She stepped backward, tripping over a large tabby cat, and squealed with fright. The cat made a horrible screeching sound, catapulting Mrs. Quinlan into action.

"OUT!" she screamed, grabbing Grace by the collar and dragging her toward the front door. The others followed close behind, yelling at the woman and trying to loosen her grip on Grace's collar.

"Please!" Grace shouted desperately. "Our friend's possessed! We don't know how to help her…"

"Little brats!" Mrs. Quinlan shrieked, still holding fast to Grace's collar. "Horrible little brats!"

"Please!" Grace begged again as she began to cry. "The spells are all happening. We did the Ouija board—ouch!—in school! Now something's making all our spells happen…and…"

Mrs. Quinlan stopped suddenly. She pulled Grace toward her and looked directly into her eyes.

"What did you say?"

"We did the Ouija board," Grace sobbed. "And now all our spells are working."

"Where?" the woman snapped, showering Grace with spit. "Where did you do the Ouija board?"

"In the P block," Grace said.

Mrs. Quinlan dropped her suddenly and rushed back into the kitchen. The girls could hear her rummaging loudly through cupboards, swearing. Then there was a loud smack on the kitchen table.

"Where?!" she yelled again.

"Let's get out of here," Adie said, pulling the others to the front door. "While we still can! She's *crazy!*"

"Get in here and show me exactly where!" the woman shouted from the kitchen.

"No," Grace said to Adie, taking her hand and nodding to the others. "Come on, let's go back."

Jenny and Rachel looked worried, but followed Grace as she led Adie back down the gloomy hallway. Mrs. Quinlan had pushed the caged cat aside and was holding a large, curly sheet of paper open on the table. She looked up at them, her eyes wide and worried.

"Show me exactly *where*," she repeated.

Grace circled the table to stand next to her and gazed at the fine-lined drawing of an H-shaped structure. Four blocks labeled *A, B, C,* and *D* connected by corridors, all leading to an area labeled "Main Hall" in the center.

"It's a blueprint of the school," she gasped. "Why do you have this?"

"Where?!" Mrs. Quinlan shouted again, banging her hand on the table for emphasis.

Scanning the diagram, Grace pointed to a blank area in the top left-hand corner, next to the C block.

"There," she said. "But these drawings are old. There's another part of the building there now, called the P Block. It's the newest part of the school."

Mrs. Quinlan sucked in a long breath between her teeth and staggered backward until she flopped into a chair.

"Oh God," she muttered. "What have you done? *What have you girls done?*"

chapter 7
baby burden

Sitting at the table in the cat-filled kitchen, Mrs. Quinlan tapped a pencil between her top and bottom teeth.

"So let me see if I've got this right," she said. "You did a bunch of spells. They didn't work. You did the Ouija board. It didn't work. You then decided that this foray into the occult was not exciting enough, so you broke into the school under cover of darkness and—"

"We didn't break in," Adie interrupted. "There was a Career Night."

"I see. So the Career Night was in that particular part of the school?"

"No, it was in the main hall and one of the other blocks."

"So how did you end up in the new part?" the woman said.

"We—"

"You sneaked!"

"Snuck," Adie frowned, sulking.

"Shut up." Mrs. Quinlan raised one finger, preventing Adie from interrupting again. "You *sneaked* into this new part of the building and promptly summoned a demon, which possessed your friend Enid—"

"Una," Grace corrected.

"And proceeded to execute each of your spells, starting with the most recent one. Do I have this right so far?"

"Yes. Although we don't know it's a demon. I mean, it's a *something*. A spirit or whatever. I'm not sure what the difference is."

"What a relief you took care to educate yourselves properly before messing with something so dangerous," Mrs. Quinlan said. "Show me this list of spells. How many are there?"

"Nine altogether," replied Grace, pulling her

notebook from her pocket and handing it over. "There are six left to go."

Mrs. Quinlan tapped the pencil against her yellowing canines and breathed loudly as she read through the list.

"Made a boy pee himself, did you?" she sneered. "What a tremendous achievement. And the snow? That was you, was it? How original. If only you girls had found the occult sooner. What a wonderful world this would be."

She read on to herself, as the girls glanced nervously at each other.

"My, my, my," Mrs. Quinlan said quietly after a moment, sitting up straight in her chair. She raised her eyes and looked at the girls carefully. "That, I wasn't expecting."

"We didn't mean it," Grace whispered. "Tracy gave Jenny a black eye and…"

"And you decided that she deserved to die."

"We didn't mean it."

"These aren't parlor tricks and practical jokes,"

Mrs. Quinlan said, leaning forward. "If you're going to cast a spell to end someone's life, you'd better be absolutely sure you mean it."

"So can you help us or not?" Jenny asked.

"You really are a charming bunch, aren't you?"

"Can you help us?" Jenny repeated.

Mrs. Quinlan took a deep breath and sat back in her chair.

"I can try," she said. "But we're dealing with powers bigger and meaner than anything you could imagine. This isn't going to be easy. There a few things we can try, but I need your solemn word that you'll do whatever I tell you. There's no chickening out now. Understood?"

"Understood," said Grace firmly. "Whatever we have to do, we'll do it."

"Good," said the woman. "Now get out of my house. I have potions to mix, and I need peace and quiet while I do it."

"Do you want to take my cell number," asked Grace, "so you can call us when you need us?"

"Do you see a phone around here?"

"Oh, then how will you get in touch with us?"

"Keep an eye on the hedge at the end of the football field," the woman replied. "I'll tie a red scarf on it when I need you."

Grace nodded in agreement. Mrs. Quinlan raised her eyebrows.

"Are you still here?"

"Sorry," said Grace. "We're leaving. And…you know…thanks."

"Hmph," was the woman's response.

Two minutes later, the girls were back in the cul-de-sac.

"I don't trust her," said Adie as they scrambled back through the wiry hedge toward school.

"Well, she's the only chance we've got, and she seems to know what she's talking about," said Grace. "Besides, it's a relief to know we're not on our own anymore."

"Maybe, but…I don't know. What's the stuff she's talking about that we can't chicken out of? What's she going to make us do?"

"Yeah," said Jenny. "What if she tells us we have to sacrifice a goat or something?"

"I'm not doing that." Adie frowned.

"Me neither," said Rachel.

"We don't know what we're going to have to do," sighed Grace. "We'll just have to hope it's nothing like that."

The group went silent as they trundled across the football field, each picturing the horrible, gross deeds that might be required to banish the demon they had summoned. Each one was already dreading the sight of a red scarf, tied to a branch of the skinny hedge, dancing in the breeze.

✳✳✳

On Friday morning, Grace arrived at her locker and was horrified to see a red rose tucked into the door. Whipping it out and stuffing it into her bag before anyone else could see, she turned—to find herself looking straight into the handsome eyes of James O'Connor.

"Good morning." He smiled.

She groaned to herself.

"Hello, James."

"I left something for you, on your locker."

"I got it, thank you."

"I was wondering if you wanted to go see a movie this weekend."

"I'm really...I'm very busy. I really can't."

Grace turned and walked quickly down the corridor. James followed, keeping in step with her.

"What about just meeting at the park?" he asked hopefully. "Just for a little bit. We could have a picnic or something."

"I don't like picnics."

"No, of course not." He nodded solemnly. "They just attract bees and stuff, don't they? What about just going for a walk then?"

"I'm really not feeling well, James," she said, stopping suddenly. "I think I'm just going to stay home this weekend."

"Good idea," he said. "I'll come over to your house."

"No!" she exclaimed. "Please don't."

"Just for a few minutes," he said. "To see how you are. I could bring some soup."

"Don't bring any soup," Grace said. "Don't bring anything. Don't come to my house. Please."

She felt a pang of guilt at the hurt look on his face.

"I'd just like to see you," he said quietly. "The weekends feel really long 'cause I don't get to see you. Monday is so far away."

"You two!" barked a passing teacher. "You're late for class. Hurry up, now."

Grace silently thanked him for the interruption.

"I'm really sorry, James," she said. "I'll see you later."

Then she took off at a jog, cursing herself for a fool.

✳✳✳

On Saturday, Grace escaped to Jenny's house, in the hope of avoiding James should he turn up at her house.

"Why didn't you just tell him you were going away for the weekend or something?" asked Jenny.

"I didn't think of that," said Grace. "I just got all nervous and wanted to run away."

Jenny smiled.

"There was a time when you would never have run from James O'Connor!"

"Yeah, well," said Grace, "that was before we made him all weird. Now he just freaks me out."

"He still has nice eyes though," Jenny said with a wink.

"Yeah, but they don't blink when he's looking at me." Grace shivered. "Makes me nervous."

"Jenny!" Jenny's mom called from the kitchen. "Can you watch the baby for a minute? I have to pop over to see Mrs. Walker."

"Coming, Mom!" Jenny called back. "Come on," she said to Grace, "you can give me a hand."

"Thanks, love," Jenny's mom said, as she handed over the drooling infant. "Won't be too long. There's microwave popcorn in the cupboard if you girls get hungry."

When Jenny was sure her mother was out of sight, she flicked on the TV to the cartoon channel.

"Mom doesn't let Sarah watch TV. She says she's too young for it. But Sarah loves it. She goes all quiet when it's on. You want some popcorn?"

Grace nodded as she laid out the play mat for the baby. Jenny plopped Sarah onto it and disappeared into the kitchen.

"Want some juice as well? We got this new mixed berry stuff. It's really nice."

"Yeah," Grace yelled back. "If you're having some—"

Grace couldn't finish the sentence. She looked at the baby, and horror washed over her. *What was Sarah doing?*

"Jenny," she whispered.

She could hear her friend switch on the microwave, and the corn began to pop.

"Jenny!" she said louder.

"I didn't hear you," Jenny called. "Did you want juice?"

"Jenny!" Grace screamed this time.

Jenny raced into the living room.

"What is it? Is it Sarah?!"

Grace nodded slowly, her eyes wide, and pointed toward the television.

Jenny's mouth fell open, and she let out a small whine of shock.

There, standing firmly on her pudgy eight-month-old legs and tapping one foot, was Jenny's baby sister. She looked back to grin at them as she flicked through the television channels, finally stopping at one showing *Finding Nemo*. She let out a squeal of delight, walked steadily back to the play mat, and sat down.

"She's walking." Grace gasped. "Walking around like a grown-up kid. Her legs don't even look like they can carry her weight yet."

"They can't," breathed Jenny. "I mean, they're not supposed to—she's too young. It's spell number six!"

After one particularly grueling afternoon of baby-sitting, Jenny had wished that her little sister could take care of herself for just one day. The girls had humored her with an appropriate spell.

"Oh, God," Jenny whispered. "I didn't think it would look like this. This is so...so *obvious*. My mom's definitely going to notice this."

"We have to hide this from your mom and dad."

"*How?*"

"Offer to babysit for the day," replied Grace. "We'll take her to my house. No, wait, not my house. Just in case you-know-who pops over. We'll take her to Adie's."

Sarah looked back at them and gurgled loudly, before getting to her feet once more and striding toward the kitchen. At that moment, they heard Jenny's mom open the back door.

"Grab her!" Grace squealed.

Jenny rushed forward, scooping Sarah up into her arms, just as her mom walked into the kitchen.

"You all right, girls?" she asked, noticing their flushed faces.

"Yeah, fine," Jenny panted.

"I'll take her now, if you guys want to head up to Jenny's room."

"No!" Jenny almost shouted. Then, calming herself, she said, "No, Mom, that's okay. I was thinking I'd give you and Dad a rest today. Why don't me and Grace take Sarah out for a while? You can have a nice, relaxing dinner this evening, by yourselves. You know, romantic, and all that."

Jenny's mom gave her a funny look.

"Really?" she said. "Well, that's very sweet of you, hon, but are you sure you girls can manage by yourselves?"

"Oh, yeah," replied Jenny. "I've a feeling she won't be any trouble today at all. Plus, I've got my cell with me so I can give you a call if I need to."

"That's very kind of you, girls." Her mom smiled back. "Your dad and I would really appreciate that. But please don't hesitate to call me, all right? About anything."

"Will do, Mom," Jenny called, as she hurried into the hall and tucked the baby into her stroller. Her mom packed up a bag of the baby's things and handed it to Jenny as she leaned in to give Sarah a kiss. Jenny exhaled loudly as she watched her mom head back into the kitchen.

"Ah!" Grace squealed. She rushed forward to grab hold of Sarah, who had unbuckled herself from the stroller and was climbing, chimpanzeelike, down one side.

"We'd better get out of here," said Jenny.

✳✳✳

"Your parents aren't here, are they?"

Adie frowned at the two girls who stood, panting, on her porch.

"And hello to you too."

"We've no time for sarcasm," Grace said, pushing past Adie into the house. "Are your parents here?"

"No, they went to my granny's. What's going on?"

"Thank goodness." Jenny sighed, wheeling the stroller inside.

"What is it?"

"It's spell number six," replied Grace. "And it's creepier than we thought it would be."

"There's a shocker," said Adie. "Everything's turning out creepier than we thought it would be. What was number six again?"

"That baby Sarah could take care of herself for a day. Well, she seems very able to do that right now. Take a look at this."

Grace lifted the baby out of the stroller and placed her gently on the floor. Sarah immediately got to her feet, stepped up onto the wheel of the stroller just long enough to grab her bottle, and trotted into the kitchen.

"Ugh!"

"Hey!" Jenny complained. "She's still my baby sister, you know."

"Sorry," Adie apologized, "but that's just plain freaky looking."

"And I'm afraid she'll have to stay here for the day," said Grace. "We have to keep her hidden from her parents, or we're all in trouble."

Just then they heard the microwave turn on in the kitchen. They rushed in to see Sarah balanced carefully on a kitchen chair, pressing buttons to heat up her bottle of milk. Jenny picked her up and opened the microwave door to switch it off. Sarah shrieked in protest.

"We can't take our eyes off her," Jenny said, "even for a second."

"I don't know," mumbled Adie, "it looked like she knew what she was doing there."

Jenny shot her a look, and Adie pursed her lips together to show she wasn't going to say any more.

"Well," said Grace, "we'd better get comfy. We're not going anywhere for a while."

chapter 8
a walk in the park

Taking care of a baby who's incapable of doing anything for herself is tiring. Taking care of a baby who's
perfectly capable of doing everything for herself is posi-
tively exhausting. The girls could barely sit down for
five minutes before Sarah would take off at a jog, looking for something else in the house to amuse her. They
watched her wipe her own mouth after drinking her
bottle, tidy her own soft toys into a neat pile at one end
of her play mat and, most disturbingly, begin to change
her own diaper before Jenny whipped her up onto the
changing mat to do it for her. Eventually, Adie found a
DVD of *Finding Nemo,* and they all collapsed onto the

sofa as the baby sat contentedly watching the screen. Grace was practically asleep when her cell rang. It was her home number.

"Grace, hon? Just wondering where you are. Are you still at Jenny's house?"

"Oh, hi, Mom. No, we're over at Adie's now. We're taking care of Sarah for the day, to give Jenny's mom and dad a rest."

"Oh, I see," her mom said. "She's actually at her friend Adie's house, James. It's just down the road."

Grace shot up in her seat.

"Mom?"

"No problem, James. See you again. That was your friend, James, Grace. From school. He seems like a nice boy."

"You didn't show him which house was Adie's, did you, Mom?"

"He's on his way over now, dear. Is there something wrong?"

Grace groaned to herself.

"No, nothing's wrong, Mom. I'll see you later."

"Let me know if you're not going to be home for dinner."

"Okay."

Grace hung up and dropped her forehead onto her knees.

"What's up?" Jenny lay sprawled out, taking up more than her fair share of the sofa.

"As if today wasn't bad enough," Grace muttered into her lap, "James O'Connor's on his way over."

"You'll have to get rid of him," Jenny said, sitting up. "Just tell him to get lost."

"I can't say that," moaned Grace. "And it wouldn't work anyway. I told him not to come to my house, and he did anyway."

"Tell him you're sick," said Adie.

"Then why would I be in your house?"

"Quarantine. You don't want to infect your mother."

"I don't think that'll work, Adie," said Grace. "Besides, it would be pretty cruel of me to avoid getting my mom sick by hanging out with an eight-month-old baby."

"True," agreed Jenny. "We're in a bit of a pickle here."

The doorbell rang. The girls froze.

"We just won't answer," Adie whispered. "He'll go away eventually."

The doorbell rang again. After a moment, they heard footsteps from the porch to the window.

"Get down!" whispered Grace.

All three dropped to their bellies on the floor, sheltered by the sofa. There was a gentle knock on the window.

"Hello?" they heard James say. "Anyone there?"

Jenny gasped and lunged to grab hold of her sister, but it was too late. Sarah had skipped onto the sofa, using Adie as a step, and was giving an enthusiastic thumbs-up to the visitor behind the glass. James slowly offered his own thumbs-up, confused by the scene but unable to put his finger on what, exactly, was wrong with it. The girls conceded defeat and stood up in full view before Sarah could do any more grown-up-baby tricks. Grace faked a smile that was more of a grimace.

"Hi!" he chirped, as she opened the front door. "Your mom told me you were over here. She's really nice. How are you doing? Feeling any better today?"

"Fine," mumbled Grace.

"Who's the baby? Is that your little sister?"

"No, Jenny's."

"I'm great with babies," said James. "Well, I'm all right with them. I've watched my little cousin a couple of times. Changed diapers and everything!"

"That's great."

"So, you know, if you guys could use a hand, I'd be happy to help out."

"Oh! No, no, don't be silly," Grace said, holding the door open as little as possible, though James could still see in through the porch glass. "You wouldn't want to waste your Saturday babysitting."

"Wouldn't be wasting it if I'm with you," he said, smiling.

She grimaced again.

"Hey, is that…is she…?" he said, glancing past her with a strange look on his face.

Grace looked back to see Sarah trotting toward them, beaming brightly.

"Jenny!" she yelled, letting go of the door to grab hold of the baby. She rushed back into living room, where Jenny was kneeling on the hearth extinguishing a small fire. Adie was planted in front of the TV with the remote control in her hand and an angry look on her face.

"I think she's a little cold," Jenny puffed.

"And wants to watch something else," grunted Adie. "She's reset the TV, and I don't know how the hell she did it."

"Here, one of you take her. James is still at the front door!" Grace hissed.

"Not anymore," said a smiling James, entering the living room. "Hello, girls. I was just telling Grace, I don't mind giving you guys a hand if you're babysitting for the day."

"No thanks," Jenny blurted out. "I'm used to watching her. I don't need any help."

"Okay," he said with a grin. "Then, are you free to go for a walk in the park, Grace?"

"Yep, she sure is," replied Jenny, grabbing hold of Sarah before she managed to wriggle out of Grace's arms onto the floor.

"What?" exclaimed Grace. "No, I'm not!"

"If you don't go out now," Jenny said pointedly, through gritted teeth, "poor James will be stuck here all day. *All day*. With *us*."

"Great," James said happily. "Let's go."

Grace managed a covert scowl at her friends as James led her to the front door.

✳✳✳

Grace was grateful for the few gray clouds that sat heavily in the sky, threatening to pour at any moment. She closed her eyes, about to wish for rain 'til she thought better of it. It wouldn't be a real spell, but still. No point tempting fate. She didn't want to end up floating home.

She smiled sporadically, at James's polite, and almost incessant, conversation, but she felt really awkward. She never talked to boys alone and didn't know what she should be talking about. He seemed to be rattling on about his dogs, how the school football team was doing this year and, oddly, his aunt Maura, who had a lot of fish. He took a deep breath and smiled shyly.

"Sorry," he said, "I've just been going on and on, but you're so quiet today. And I'm a little nervous."

That surprised her and also made her feel a little less nervous. She smiled back and apologized.

"Me too," she said. "I'm a little shy, sometimes, I guess."

"I know what you mean. Bashful, my mom calls me. You know, like the dwarf in *Snow White*."

"You?" She frowned at him. "But you're really popular in school. You make lots of noise in class, and no one ever picks on you."

"I'm great when I'm with my friends." He shrugged. "But when I'm not, I get all quiet. Like you are today."

She smiled and glanced at her feet. A few small drops of rain had landed on her shoes.

"I think it's going to pour," she said.

"Yeah," he replied, "doesn't look good. Look, there's a bench over there under those trees."

They headed for shelter, just reaching the bench in time before the rain began pelting down. They sat quietly, watching the downpour, and listening as it rustled through the trees.

"I love days like these," Grace said.

"You love getting stuck in the rain?"

"Well, no," she said with a little giggle. "But when you're cozy indoors, and it's torrential outside. I like that."

"But you're not cozy indoors," he teased. "And we might be going home with pneumonia today."

"True." She smiled.

Just then there was a flash of lightning and thunder rumbled in the sky. Grace looked up and grinned even wider.

"And I *love* thunder and lightning!" she exclaimed. "How far away do you think it is?"

"Wait for another flash," he said, "then count."

After a few moments another burst of light lit up the cloudy sky, followed quickly by another deep rumble of thunder.

"Six miles!"

"Eight!" James yelled at the same time.

They looked at each other and laughed.

"I'm not sure the counting thing really works," she said.

"Apparently not," he agreed.

"Everything's so gray," she said. "It feels like we're in an old-fashioned horror movie or something."

"Maybe a headless horseman will come galloping through those trees any minute."

James leaned forward, staring intently at a clump of trees in front of them. He was quiet so long that Grace leaned forward to follow his gaze. Suddenly, he reached up, pulled down the branch above them, and shook it over Grace's head, shrieking at the same time.

"Agghh!" she screamed, jumping to her feet and into the rain.

James let go of the branch and laughed out loud.

"Very funny!" she said, mock-serious, as she ducked back under the shelter and slapped his arm.

"Sorry," he said, still laughing. "I couldn't resist. Here."

He took off his jacket and put it around her shoulders. Grace didn't object. The extra warmth felt wonderful.

"Thanks."

"No problem. Don't want you coming down with flu or something."

"Yeah, my mom would have a fit."

"So," he said, blushing a little. "I was thinking we could go see a movie tomorrow. There's lots of good stuff at the Omniplex. That new scary movie's supposed to be fantastic."

"Maybe," she said, blushing a little herself.

"Cool," he replied. "Would hate to think I wouldn't get to see you again 'til Monday."

She frowned and pulled his jacket a little tighter around herself.

"Going a whole day without seeing you is horrible," he continued.

"Really?" she said, staring straight ahead.

"Yeah," he replied. "I know we've been in the same grade forever, but I just didn't really appreciate you until now."

"Um-hm."

"It just dawned on me a couple of weeks ago. I just woke up one morning, and I couldn't wait to see you. And it's been like that ever since."

"Right."

Grace stood up and took off James's jacket.

"I'm really sorry, James," she said, handing it back to him. "But I have to get home. My mom'll be wondering where I am."

"Already? Oh. Okay." He was clearly disappointed.

"And I won't be able to go to a movie tomorrow."

"What? But I thought—"

"Sorry, James," Grace said, feeling suddenly rather choked. "I just can't."

She didn't wait for him to argue. Walking quickly in the pouring rain, the water on the ground splashed around her, soaking her feet. Her hair stuck to her face in long, dark streaks. For one happy minute, she had totally forgotten about the love spell. For one minute, she had been having a great time with the cutest boy in school, whom she'd always liked.

But James O'Connor didn't like her. Not really. And as soon as she and her friends banished the demon and stopped the spells, he would go back to not knowing she ever existed.

chapter 9
the demon well

Monday morning had held on to the weekend's gray clouds. The girls stood together on the football field, shivering against the cold, and staring at the bare hedge at the end of the field. No red scarf.

"This is stupid," said Jenny. "She's forgotten. I bet she can't even do magic."

"We'll just give her more time," Grace said. "She's our only hope."

"It's been nearly four days," Adie grumbled. "How long do we wait?"

"Just 'til the end of the day. If there's still no scarf, then…"

"Then what?" said Jenny.

"Then we'll go sit in her garden with the cats 'til it drives her crazy and she *has* to help us," said Grace.

"All right." Rachel sighed. "Who's got the non-Una this morning?"

They all groaned in unison.

"I forgot she was back from suspension," said Adie. "Do we still have to watch her? I mean, Tracy took a good punching. Maybe she'll leave her alone now."

"We can't risk it," replied Rachel. "I'd say the Beast has even more reason to go after her now."

"But, even if she does, should we worry?" asked Adie, totally serious. "I mean, the non-Una seemed able to handle her. Much more than all of us together. If Tracy goes for her again, she'll get her lights punched out."

"How is that any better?" said Rachel. "When we get the real Una back, she'll find out she's been expelled and is on her way to prison, or juvenile prison, or wherever they send kid criminals."

"Good point."

"I'll take first shift," offered Jenny.

"Good," said Grace. "See you all at break."

✳✳✳

In history class that afternoon, Adie doodled flowers and birds on her notebook as Grace tried, in vain, to pay attention to Mr. McQuaid's droning voice.

"And it was the stopping of the mail coaches that was to signal the start of the 1798 Rebellion. Do you all have that down?"

Grace jotted down a few words, but by the time she had reached the end of the sentence, she had already forgotten what it was.

"But the uprising was doomed from the beginning," the teacher went on. "In fact, cheese was aware of the curtains due to an egg in the spaceship."

Grace's eyes snapped to the teacher, and Adie's hand froze, mid-scribble. A small titter of confused laughter rippled across the classroom. Mr. McQuaid stood still for a moment, looking perplexed, then tried to continue.

"The rebels ate chalk, and cowboy shoes melt concrete finishing flowers."

He stood still again, waiting for more of the bewildered laughter to die down. He opened his mouth, then closed it again. Rubbing his chin and swallowing a few times in quick succession, he tried again.

"Quake but rainbow remote control…no…piddling takes charming noodles around the mountain and…ah!"

Mr. McQuaid shook his head vigorously and rubbed his eyes. The laughter had now trebled in volume, and the whole class watched him, open-eyed, waiting for another deluge of nonsense.

"Peter the Rabbit, *brrrrr*—" He clapped his hand over his mouth, shook his head again, and sprinted for the door.

Students raced to the doorway to watch him hurry down the hallway, then huddled in groups inside and outside the classroom, talking excitedly about how Mr. McQuaid had gone crazy. Grace and Adie stayed in their seats, not looking at the other students or each other. Grimly, Grace pulled the notebook out of her bag, flipped through the pages, and made a little mark beside spell number five: "Make Mr. McQuaid talk gobbledygook in history."

"Only four more to go," Adie whispered through trembling lips.

"Come on," said Grace, pulling her bag onto the table and packing up her things, "we need to check the hedge."

They slipped through their classmates, careful not to be seen by any teachers as they snuck outside. Hunkering down, almost crawling, they passed classroom windows and headed to the end of the building. The cold wind whipped at their cheeks, making them glow bright pink. Grace hugged her jacket tightly around her, closing her eyes as they turned the corner to the football field. *This is it*, she thought, *if it's not there, we're back to square one.* She squeezed her eyes shut even tighter, then opened them slowly.

There, tied to one wiry, bare branch and fluttering in the breeze, was a deep crimson scarf.

✳✳✳

The four girls watched as Mrs. Quinlan wrestled a large rolled-up sheet of paper out of a basket of junk in one corner of her kitchen.

"First of all," the woman said, "let me explain what you've gotten yourselves into."

She unfurled the blueprint of the school and stabbed her finger into the point where the new school block had been built.

"This here," she said, "is the site of a demon well. A very rare occurrence on our plane, and a very danger-ous one. It's like a weak spot in the Earth's crust, but on a spiritual level. Demons can push through onto our plane and take possession of animals, objects, or silly schoolgirls."

"Then how come there aren't tons of possessed kids in school?" asked Jenny.

"If you shut up and listen, you'll find out. A demon can push through onto our plane, but only through a suitable medium. The conductor of a séance, for example, or a—"

"Or a Ouija board," said Grace.

"Sweet lord, the girl's some sort of genius! Yes, a Ouija board. And *you*, idiot children, were kind enough to provide that suitable medium. *Hey presto*, a demon snuck up through the ether, grabbed hold of your friend, what's-her-name, and began wreaking a little havoc."

"But why make our spells work?" said Jenny.

"Couldn't say. Demons are mischievous. You never know what they'll get up to and why. The notebook was lying open by the board, you say? I guess it was in a playful mood and sensed some meager attempts at magic nearby. Now it's flexing its magic muscles."

"So how do we stop it?" asked Adie.

"Calm yourself there, Amy—"

"Adie."

"I'm getting to that. There are a number of things we could try, but the quickest and the safest would be to push from the demon end. Trap your friend in a circle and expel the demon."

"Like an exorcism?" said Jenny.

"Of sorts. But with a pathway included, so it doesn't possess anything else."

"How does that work?" said Grace.

Mrs. Quinlan rolled her eyes and sighed.

"Working with a group of twits is really quite exhausting. The enchantment includes a *pathway*. Instead of banishing the demon in any old direction—"

"Where it could grab onto another one of us," Jenny interrupted.

"Thank you, Mrs. Helpful-Pants. Yes, instead of sending it off any which way, you stick it to a pathway that goes straight down the well."

"And what's to stop it from coming back up?" asked Grace.

"Well, Greta—"

"Grace."

"Unless you're planning another of your lovely Ouija sessions at that very spot, then it can't come back up, can it?"

"Good," Grace said, suddenly smiling. "Better than good, that's great! We're going to make everything right!"

"Hold your horses there, Sparky," said Mrs. Quinlan, rolling up the blueprint. "This isn't going to be a walk in the park. That demon may be playing the part of the schoolgirl right now, but it's not going to like being trapped in a circle. You'll have to be very quick and very careful. Get the circle around it before it realizes what's going on."

"We've already seen what it does when it gets mad." Adie shuddered.

"Indeed?"

"It punched the school bully square in the face for pinning it up against the wall."

"That's nothing," said the woman. "Wait 'til it realizes you're trying to kick it out of this realm entirely. That'll really make it mad."

"Are you going to help us with the enchantment?" asked Grace.

"Hey," said Mrs. Quinlan, raising a finger. "I'm giving you the tools and the information, but I'm not going to risk my neck for you all. *You've* made this mess. *You* clean it up."

***

The girls agreed that Tuesday, after school, was when Mrs. Quinlan's exorcism enchantment would take place. Rachel was sent to lure the non-Una to the P block, while the others waited there in preparation.

"Ugh!" Adie exclaimed, sniffing inside the cookie jar Mrs. Quinlan had given them. "This stuff stinks! Wonder what's in it."

"I wouldn't ask," replied Grace.

"And how are we supposed to get it all over the non-Una without her noticing?"

"We'll have to do it stealthy like," said Grace.

"And quickly," warned Jenny. "Before she starts wondering where the smell is coming from."

Grace had drawn a circle in salt over their Ouija board spot, but left it open a few inches. When the non-Una stepped inside the circle, Grace was to close up the gap with salt as quickly as possible. Jenny held a scrap of paper, scribbled with Mrs. Quinlan's untidy writing, in her shaking hands.

"Here they come!" said Adie.

"Hello, girls," the non-Una said, with her usual

wide-eyed weirdness. "Rachel says we're going to do some homework here together."

"That's right," replied Adie, her hands working deftly behind her back and lifting the lid off the cookie jar containing the magic goo.

"No teachers left in the school," Rachel whispered to Grace, "but we'll have to keep an eye out for the janitor."

Grace and Jenny smiled pleasantly at the non-Una, as they inched forward to scoop a handful each of the foul-smelling concoction.

"We thought we'd use one of the empty labs, where it's quiet." Jenny put her hand on the non-Una's back and surreptitiously wiped the dark gray slime down her sweater.

"It's quiet *here*," the non-Una said, smiling back.

"Three," Grace said quietly.

"And there's ample lighting," the non-Una continued.

"Two."

"But are we allowed to be here after hours?"

"One."

"Hmm?"

"*Now!*" screamed Grace.

Rachel grabbed the non-Una's wrist and flung her toward the circle. Grace gave her another push as she smeared more of the gray gloop under her throat, then fell to her knees to complete the circle of salt.

"Now! Do it now, Jenny!" yelled Grace.

Jenny held the paper and shouted at the top of her voice:

> "*Return, Demon, from whence you came,*
> *Abandon, now, your evil game,*
> *This sparkling realm is not your own,*
> *Return, this instant, to your home!*"

The non-Una gave a howling shriek, her eyes turning as red as blood. Grace fell backward as a powerful gust of wind swept through the hall, churning up litter and dust in a mini-tornado above the circle. The girls scrambled back to the double doors, holding on to each other in desperation as a sudden darkness descended on the hall.

Everything went very, very quiet.

"Is it over?" Adie whispered.

No one answered. They watched as the darkness began to lift.

At the end of the hall, there were two flecks of glowing red.

"Oh God!" whispered Grace. "It didn't work."

The last of the darkness dissolved to reveal the non-Una on all fours, panting as if out of breath. She was glaring at them with burning, furious eyes and inching slowly forward.

"Run!" screamed Jenny. "*Run!*"

Springing to their feet, the girls raced down the corridor, hearing the pounding feet of the creature behind them. Metal trash bins and other debris from the school halls were fired at them from behind, one grazing Rachel's arm and another Jenny's leg. The girls whimpered and squealed in terror, pulling each other along. As they rounded the corner into the A block, the long wall of lockers to their left began to rock—and slowly tip forward.

"*Look out!*" Grace screamed, dragging Adie to safety. Jenny and Rachel ducked out of the way of the falling wall of metal just in time.

The girls collapsed in a heap on the floor. They looked up to see the non-Una standing at one end of the fallen lockers, grinning, as they sat, trapped, at the other. Adie's left hand still held fast to Mrs. Quinlan's cookie jar. With tears streaming down her face, she stood up and flung the tin with all her might.

"Take that, you freak!"

The jar bounced off the demon's head with a horrible clang and showered it with the remains of the rank-smelling paste. The non-Una made a face and stepped back. Then, wiping its cheek with the sleeve of its sweater, it smiled its creepy half smile, calmly turned, and walked away.

The girls remained still, trying to catch their breath.

"Is she gone?" Adie wheezed. "I mean, is *it* gone?"

"Who's down there?" a voice boomed suddenly from the other end of the corridor. "Who's making all that racket down there? I'm calling the police!"

"The janitor!" Rachel hissed. "Let's get out of here!"

They clambered to their feet and almost fell through one of the classroom doors. Sliding across desks and over chairs, they barreled through the emergency exit, setting off the fire alarm.

"Keep running!" shouted Grace.

With one mind, the girls pelted across the football field until they finally came to a breathless halt at the bare hedge separating the school from Wilton Place.

✳✳✳

Mrs. Quinlan frowned at the four girls in various stages of collapse on her porch step.

"I take it plan A didn't work then," she said.

"No," Grace puffed, "it didn't work."

"Hmm," the woman mused. "I suppose you'd better come in. Wipe your feet."

Mrs. Quinlan poured out four very strong cups of tea and sat down heavily in her chair.

"Just what I was afraid of," she muttered. "The

demon's a powerful one. Well, in that case, on to plan B."

"And what will that involve?" snapped Jenny. "More of trying to get us killed?"

"Don't be such a drama queen. You're still breathing, aren't you?"

"Only just."

"Then quit your bellyaching. I warned you it was going to be no walk in the park when we started this. So suck it up and listen."

Jenny scowled and sipped her tea.

"We'll have to try it from the well end," said the woman. "A little more dangerous and a little more complicated. But necessary."

"*More* dangerous!" Grace exclaimed. "That demon was going to kill us!"

"Honestly"—Mrs. Quinlan sighed, exasperated— "such a bunch of whiners I never met."

Grace snorted loudly in what was half an exclamation of disbelief and half a laugh.

"If you want to get rid of this thing," the woman

said pointedly, "then this is the next step. It's an incantation to make the mouth of the well a…a kind of vacuum."

"A *vacuum*?" said Grace.

"Which will suck back any beings from its own realm."

"Nice," said Jenny. "And I suppose this means we have to, somehow, get the non-Una back on top of the well?"

"She'll never do it," Adie interrupted, "not after today."

"Was I finished?" the woman asked. "No, you do not have to get what's-her-face back to the well for this one. As long as she's sort of in the vicinity, the demon will get sucked in."

"How *sort of*?" asked Grace.

"When she's in the building. Do it during school hours."

"We'll get caught," said Rachel. "How can we do it without running into any teachers?"

"I guess you'll have to use your immense brainpower

and find a way to do it *without* getting caught," Mrs. Quinlan replied.

"You said this way was more dangerous," Grace cut in. "What's more dangerous about it?"

The woman took a deep breath through her nose and looked squarely at Grace.

"You were dealing with one demon before. By altering the state of the well temporarily, which is what you will be doing, you mess with its permeability."

She glanced around at four confused faces.

"It will intermittently become easier for demons to get through."

The faces remained confused, and Mrs. Quinlan sighed loudly.

"There will be moments during the incantation," she said slowly, as if addressing a group of small children, "when the well will become more permeable than it is at present. If there is a demon nearby at one of these moments, it may be able to slip through."

"So we could conceivably have a number of demons

slipping through during the whole incantation," said Grace, alarmed.

"Conceivably, yes."

"Then we can't possibly risk it! What if we all get possessed?"

"Oh, I hadn't thought of that," said Mrs. Quinlan, mockingly putting her finger to her lip. "Look. I'll give you potions and charms to protect yourselves, *obviously*. But you'll have to use them immediately, and make sure those demons go straight back down the well. No running like scaredy-cats at the first sign of trouble. And that includes *you*."

She pointed at Adie, who opened her mouth in mute protest.

"Right," the Old Cat Lady said, "get lost, all of you. I now have tons of work to do. Have I thanked you for that yet, by the way? Thank you. Thanks so much."

"When will—"

"Look out for the red scarf."

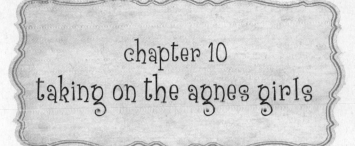

chapter 10
taking on the agnes girls

School, the next morning, was buzzing with excitement. Everyone had heard rumors that the A block had been destroyed by vandals the night before.

"I heard they set it on fire," said one girl, her eyes twinkling at the thought.

"No way," said another. "I saw it this morning, and there's no way it was on fire."

"Heard the lockers got trashed, though. My big brother's locker is in that block and he said no one could get in to get their books. They were told to go without them for the day."

"Cool! I'm gonna tell all my teachers my locker's in the A block. No homework for me today!"

Grace frowned as she pushed through the crowds to her own locker. The others were already waiting for her.

"We're famous." Jenny tried to lighten the mood, but her face was anything but happy.

"Good morning, girls."

"Aaaggh!" Adie screeched, causing everyone in the block to turn and look at them. The non-Una had appeared right beside them, unperturbed as always.

"Those girls are so weird," Grace heard one voice in the crowd mumble before the excited chattering began again.

"G-good morning, Una," Grace stammered.

"Good morning, Grace," said the non-Una. "Everyone looking forward to the game this afternoon?"

"Yep," said Jenny.

"Wonderful." The non-Una smiled and headed toward her locker, leaving the girls to sink against the wall.

"Isn't she going to do something?" asked Adie. "Isn't she going to, you know, try and kill us or something?"

"Apparently not," breathed Grace.

"I take it we're not on Una-duty anymore," said Rachel.

"I don't think so," answered Grace. "She'll have to fend for herself against Tracy, or Tracy will have to fend for *her*self…. Either way, I'm not chaperoning anymore. I'm too scared."

"Me too," Adie agreed.

"Me three," said Jenny. "If Una ends up getting expelled, we'll deal with that then. In the meantime, she's on her own."

"Oh, fudge," Grace said suddenly, pulling Adie in front of her and ducking down.

"What? Is she back?" Adie whispered.

"No. James O'Connor."

"This is getting ridiculous," Jenny said, stepping forward to help keep Grace covered. "You're spending half your time hiding behind lockers and ducking under tables. You can't avoid him forever."

"I can try. Move away from my locker, everyone together, just in case."

The other three shuffled sideways, all facing forward, while Grace crept along behind them.

"Ooh," Adie gasped. "He is going for your locker!"

"I'm thinking that's a love letter he's sticking in the door." Grace could hear the smile in Jenny's voice.

"Oh God, did anyone see?"

"Yep, everyone."

"Thanks for lying so I wouldn't get embarrassed. Can we leave now?"

"Yeah. Looks like he's going to wait by your locker for a while. Probably thinking you have to show up sometime. When he's looking the other direction, we'll all run, on three. Ready? One, two…"

Grace couldn't wait and scurried up the corridor with the others on her heels.

Later that day, in the gym, Adie pulled at the collar of her polo shirt.

"I hate our PE gear. It never fits right. And why does it have to be this horrible maroon color?"

"For optimum humiliation," replied Grace.

The girls were slightly out of breath after walking

(not *running*, as instructed) down the hill from school and back again. Now, the real humiliation would begin. Jenny was the only one in their group who was any good at sports, and even she wasn't great at basketball. But once a week, along with their classmates, the girls were subjected to a grueling and embarrassing mini-tournament. If only Ms. Woods hadn't left. She had always been perfectly content to sit and do crosswords while the students wandered around playing a slow game of badminton here or an even slower game of tennis there. The new PE teacher, Mr. O'Dwyer, wasn't so laid-back. He insisted on lengthy runs to warm up followed by competitive sports that were to be taken very seriously. Lately, his torment of choice for the girls was the dreaded b-ball.

"Right, girls!" Mr. O'Dwyer yelled before giving one sharp, shrill blow of his whistle. "Let's pick teams."

Grace groaned. Jenny would be picked quickly enough. Grace, Adie, and Rachel would be among the last to be chosen.

"Um," Kelly Daly paused, dissatisfied at the disappointing choice left to her. "Rachel, I guess."

"Thanks for the enthusiasm," Rachel muttered under her breath as she stood up to join Kelly's team.

"Adie," Charlotte Wynn sighed.

"That leaves Grace on Kelly's team," Mr. O'Dwyer said helpfully.

"Let the pain begin," Grace quipped, shooting Rachel a quick glance.

Ten minutes in and Charlotte's team were already up six points. Kelly was shouting furious instructions to her team, which included ordering Grace and Rachel to give the ball a wide berth.

"If it does get passed to you, give it straight to me or Melissa."

"Yes, ma'am," Rachel sneered, giving Kelly's back a big fake salute. "She's such a bossy cow. This isn't just *her* game. So what if we don't win?"

"I don't care if we win or not," Grace said wearily. "I just want to hear the final whistle."

Just then, Charlotte Wynn swooped past them,

dribbling the ball and heading straight for the basket. Rachel pursed her lips in determination and lunged forward. With alarming skill, she swiped the ball from Charlotte, spun around, letting it bounce between her legs, and charged to the other end of the court.

Grace watched in astonishment as Rachel leaped into the air, grabbed hold of the rim of the basket, and dunked the ball. Dropping to her feet with athletic grace, Rachel stared upward, openmouthed, as the girls around her fell silent.

"Spectacular!" Mr. O'Dwyer shouted excitedly, clapping his hands. "Fantastic, Rachel, that was pure genius. How come we haven't seen moves like that from you before?"

A sly smile crept across Rachel's face.

"Think I was just holding back a little, sir," she replied, grinning.

"Well, no more of that, young lady," he said, clapping again. "Play on!"

The game resumed, and before they knew it, Rachel's newfound sporting talents had catapulted her team into the lead. She scored point after point. There was barely a moment when she didn't have control of the ball.

"Enjoying yourself?" Grace asked drily, during halftime.

"Sure am," said Rachel, looking very pleased. "Have you seen Kelly Daly's face? She's fuming!"

"Well, don't get used to it," Grace warned. "That's spell number four—and it's of the temporary sort."

"Are you sure?" Rachel asked, looking a little deflated.

"Instead of being the basketball dunce,
Rachel would like to be winner, for once.

"Isn't that how it went?" said Grace.

"Ah, fudge. Never mind. It's fun while it lasts!"

Rachel playfully slapped Grace's arm as she bounced back onto the court for the second half.

"A triumph!" cheered Mr. O'Dwyer when the game was over. "Rachel, you've really got an awesome talent there. Though, everyone did well, of course."

Rachel patted Kelly on the back and smiled.

"Yeah," she said, "you *all* did well."

Kelly snarled and shrugged off Rachel's hand.

"In fact," O'Dwyer continued, "I want Rachel to be our secret weapon against Saint Agnes's in the league game tonight."

"But she's not even on the school team, sir!" Kelly objected.

"She is *now*," the teacher said. "How about it, Rachel? You up for showing Saint Agnes's a thing or two?"

"Sure, why not?" Rachel beamed.

"What are you *doing*?" Grace hissed, pulling her to one side as Kelly and the others continued to voice their objections to Mr. O'Dwyer.

"What?" Rachel said innocently. "It's just one game."

"This isn't a joke! That spell working for you means there are just two more to go before the Beast gets flattened by a bus."

"Yeah, but until the old lady sticks a scarf on the hedge, there's nothing we can do about that, is there?

What's the harm in having a little fun with one of these spells in the meantime?"

"I don't like this," said Grace.

"Neither do I," said Adie, appearing behind them.

"I promise," said Rachel, with her hand over her heart. "If the red scarf shows up before the game, I won't play. But, for the first and only time, I've got a chance to be the star of the school basketball team!"

"For one game," said Grace.

"I'll take it," Rachel declared. "You all will come along to cheer, won't you?"

She looked hopefully at the other two as they exchanged glances.

"Of course we will," Grace sighed.

"Hooray! Thanks, you guys."

"What's going on?" Jenny jogged toward them from the other end of the hall. "Someone told me you're on the team tonight."

"Yep," Rachel said. "And I'm gonna be awesome!"

✳✳✳

Saint Agnes was one of the best teams in the league, and they were known for playing dirty. Saint John's hated playing them. It always resulted in at least one injury on their side. But this particular game was going extremely well. Rachel repeated that afternoon's deft performance, running circles around the Saint Agnes girls and scoring point after point. After a while, she even began to show a little boredom with the ease of the game. So she added in jumps and spins, tricks with the ball, delighting the crowd, which cheered continuously, chanting her name and clapping wildly.

"How about letting one of us have the ball, for a change?" Kelly growled at her as the whistle for half-time blew.

"I'd love to, Kelly," Rachel replied nonchalantly, "but I'd really like to win this game. Maybe a little later, when we're enough points ahead."

"We're way ahead *now*."

Rachel winked and smiled.

"We'll see, okay?"

"Hey, Roach, or whatever your name is," sneered

the hefty captain of the Saint Agnes team, "we're going to finish you off in the second half."

"Looking forward to it," said Rachel, waving one hand in the air like a queen addressing her subjects. "I take it you weren't trying in the first half, seeing as I'm wiping the floor with you."

The captain screwed up her reddening face in fury and snarled in reply. Rachel laughed and shook her head before turning to bask in the continuing cheers of the ecstatic home crowd. She trotted over to her friends in the first row and grinned widely.

"How cool is this?!"

Jenny laughed, but Grace shook her head.

"I'd watch it, if I were you," she cautioned. "That Agnes captain looks about ready to rip your head off."

"Ah, what can she do?" Rachel said with a dismissive wave. "I'll rack up a record score in the second half, and she'll go home and lick her wounds. It's only a game, after all."

"Not sure she'd agree with you. Just be careful out there, okay?"

"No need," replied Rachel, jogging backward toward the court. "I'm on fire today!"

"Just hope you don't get burned," Grace mumbled to herself.

"What are you so worried about?" asked Jenny. "It's going great. You know, since this whole thing started, this is first time a spell has actually gone right for us. Look at Rach—she's having a ball!"

"I guess so." Grace shrugged.

"Don't be such a worrywart."

The cheers from the crowd began again, in earnest, as the whistle blew signaling the start of the second half. Naturally, Rachel had control of the ball within seconds. She darted in and out of reach of the Agnes girls, teasing them and laughing uproariously as they stumbled trying to catch up with her. As she flew past, the Agnes captain rushed at her, slamming into her shoulder. Rachel faltered momentarily before quickly recovering and going on to score another point.

"Hey, ref!" Jenny yelled. "What was *that*? That was an out-and-out foul!"

"How did she miss that?" Grace said.

"Doesn't matter," Adie said. "Hasn't slowed Rachel down at all."

And Rachel didn't look at all perturbed as the Agnes girls now seemed determined to take her down, regardless of the rules. They charged at her, one by one, but Rachel's lightning-fast feet rushed her out of harm's way each time. The ref was perplexed, ready to blow her whistle at any moment, but each seemingly inevitable foul was prevented by Rachel's incredible speed.

"You're done for, Roach," the Agnes captain bellowed, as she closed in on Rachel once more.

Rachel simply grinned in reply but, as she bounced the ball between her legs, her hand unexpectedly missed it on the return. It flew upward, catching her on the chin with such force that she stumbled, tripped, and kicked the ball right out of the court. She slid to a stop on her knees, wincing with pain as her skin was grazed badly.

"Uh-oh," said Grace.

The crowd was suddenly quiet, disappointed by the abrupt break in the spectacular sporting feats. Rachel was equally disappointed but climbed to her feet seemingly determined to continue.

"Say you're hurt," Grace muttered to herself. "A sprained ankle. Say you've a sprained ankle. *Come on*, Rach!"

But even if Rachel had heard her friend, Grace knew she wouldn't have conceded. She was obviously having far too much fun being queen of the court, and she wasn't about to give in. She ignored the Agnes captain's crooked sneer and got back into the game.

But, within minutes, it was clear that the spell had run its course. Rachel became red-cheeked and sweating as she fumbled the ball again and again. The fickle, embittered crowd started booing. Her own team, delighted by her sudden ineptitude, constantly passed her the ball, triggering one embarrassing blunder after another and more points for the opposing team.

Even worse than Saint John's team not caring about the score was the fact that the Agnes team seemed determined to settle an entirely different score altogether. Led by their relentless captain, they took every opportunity to plow into Rachel at full speed, knocking her to the ground countless times and earning stern words and occasional foul calls from the referee. But still the carnage continued.

By the time the referee announced an ultimatum, threatening to end the game if there was any more roughhousing, Rachel was a quivering wreck. She barely heard the whistle to restart play, only focusing on the wall of Agnes players that rushed toward her when it was too late. Kelly had kindly tossed the ball at her, which bounced off her stomach, before the Agnes captain barreled into her, landing heavily on top of her as Rachel hit the floor. The rest of the team followed suit, and soon she was buried, gasping for air, beneath the snickering pile of girls. The referee gave the whistle a final, piercing blow.

Smiling widely as the referee and Mr. O'Dwyer shouted stern words about the importance of safety during inter-school games, the Agnes girls got to their feet and strolled leisurely to the locker rooms, leaving Rachel lying still, and sobbing, on the ground. Grace and the others ran to their injured friend.

"God, Rachel, are you okay?" Grace said, gently taking her friend's arm and helping her to her feet.

"I think so," Rachel sniffed, cradling one side of her face. "Think my knee's sprained. And my face got a good hit."

A painful welt was already emerging on Rachel's cheek.

"You all right, Rachel?" Mr. O'Dwyer said flatly, coming over to inspect her wounds.

"Hurt my leg, sir," she said, attempting to smile. "I don't think I'll be able to stay on the team."

"Oh, eh, that's okay. We'll, eh, we'll have to manage without you. Make sure you get some ice on that bruise, okay?"

"How relieved was he?" Rachel muttered as he walked off. "Now that I'm garbage at basketball again."

"Not to worry," said Jenny brightly. "You still had your day in the sun, didn't you?"

"Half a game," Rachel said, still holding her swelling cheek. "I had half a game in the sun and then I got humiliated in front of the *whole* school. It's not fair."

"No, it's not," Grace agreed. "But what *has* been fair since this whole nightmare started? I'm really sorry, Rach. I hope you're not too upset."

"I'll live," Rachel groaned, catching a glimpse of her swollen face in the gym office window. "But no concealer's going to cover up *that*. Come on. Let's get out of here. I'll get changed at home. Don't want to run into that ogre from Saint Agnes. Or anyone from our team, come to think of it."

"Sure. I'll get your stuff," said Grace.

She ran ahead to the changing room, leaving Adie and Jenny to escort their limping friend out of the gym.

chapter 11
purple goo in
the p block

The next two days turned out to be the worst, so far, since the whole sorry business had begun. Rachel fended off abuse from Kelly and the rest of the basketball team, not to mention random students who had watched her stellar performance turn dismal on the court. Grace continued to deflect the blind affections of James O'Connor, who appeared to be getting more and more upset by her endless rejections. And all four of the girls avoided the spine-chilling politeness of the non-Una, certain that at any moment she would drop the façade, not to mention another wall of lockers.

By Friday afternoon, they were utterly exhausted.

"I can't do this anymore," Adie moaned. "How long is this going to go on? Where's the red scarf?"

"I don't know," Grace replied. "But I'm not looking forward to seeing it. Opening a well full of demons? I can wait a lifetime before having to do that."

"I'd rather that than this," Adie said. "This waiting is horrible. And everyone at school hates us now, since the basketball game."

"Thanks," said Rachel.

"Sorry."

"I'm with Adie." Jenny sighed, leaning heavily against the wall. "I just want to get this over with."

"Well, then," said Grace, "let's go check the hedge."

They walked out together to the football field. The red scarf was there at last, flapping crazily in the breeze. The girls pushed their way through the hedge, untying the scarf as they went.

The door in Wilton Place was left ajar. They went straight in and down the hall to the kitchen where the Old Cat Lady stood waiting.

"All righty," said Mrs. Quinlan, leaning both hands on the table. "Let's begin."

"It looks complicated," said Jenny, eyeing the selection of small cloth bags and porcelain containers laid out in front of her.

"It *is* complicated," replied the woman. "So pay attention. If you mess this up, you're in big trouble."

"There's no need to get mad at us," Adie whined. "We'll do the best we can."

"I mean you're in big trouble with the *demons*, twit, not *me*. Leave your brain at home, did you?"

"Sorry."

"Can I go on now?" said Mrs. Quinlan. "Or are there going to be any more pointless interruptions?"

She paused for a moment, then nodded and returned to the matter at hand.

"First of all, we have some banishing potions. They're the ones in the little cloth bags. As I said before, for the duration of the incantation, up until the very end when the well mouth becomes a Dyson, the occasional demon may be slipping through. Before it grabs hold of someone in this realm, it's not very strong. It can be banished quite easily by showering it in this stuff."

She picked up one of the bags and held it at either end of the bow that kept it tied shut.

"In order to administer the potion, one grabs hold of the bag like so, forcefully pulling apart these two ties. The bundle will open, and the powder inside will disperse, hopefully all over your demon, which will then be banished back home. Try and aim it well, and don't get any of the powder in your eyes. All clear so far?"

The girls nodded solemnly.

"If you are slow and stupid, which my experience of you tells me you are, and you fail to banish the demon at this early stage, it may succeed in grabbing hold of one of you. We then move on to the porcelain cups."

Grace gulped and took a deep breath, paying close attention to the woman's instructions.

"Full possession is a process that can take up to a minute. One can spot a person possessed by the eyes, which take on an unusual and luminous color. During these crucial seconds, the demon is not yet properly seated and can be ejected by the use of this clever little potion. Smash the container at the unfortunate person's feet and repeat the word *exitus* three times."

"That doesn't sound too difficult," said Rachel.

"The *difficult* part of this procedure is ensuring that the potion is inhaled by the subject. When thrown to the ground, the potion sublimates into a thin smoke. The subject must be held still over this smoke until it is, at least, partially inhaled. When the eyes have returned to their normal color, the demon has been evacuated."

"What happens," Grace asked tentatively, "if we don't get the subject to inhale the smoke before the demon is…properly *seated?*"

"Then, my dear, you have doubled your trouble. You'll be down one useless, stupid schoolgirl, and up one scary possessed demon-child."

"Oh."

"And now to the main event."

Mrs. Quinlan opened a cupboard behind her and

pulled out a large bowl, filled to the brim with a dark purple substance, of which the girls could already catch an unpleasant whiff.

"Ick!" said Rachel. "It smells *gross!*"

"Well, get used to it," said the woman, planting the bowl in the center of the table and securing a Tupperware lid over it, "because you'll be covering your face and hands in this stuff."

"*What?!* Why?"

"Because that's what the incantation requires. You four become the poles—north, south, east, and west—you become the mechanics of the changing state of the well mouth. So to speak."

"Fantastic," said Jenny.

"I have prepared the necessary verse, to be spoken by the North Pole," said Mrs. Quinlan.

"We have to go to the Arctic?" exclaimed Adie, confused.

"To be spoken by the *person* who *represents* the North Pole," said Mrs. Quinlan through gritted teeth. "You're giving me a headache."

"I see," said Adie, red-faced.

"Here's a small diagram outlining the necessary positions you each have to take around the mouth of the well," the woman continued. "Smear the concoction on your faces and hands, say the verse, and wait for the incantation to run its course."

"And deal with any demons that pop out in the meantime." Grace frowned.

"Indeedio."

"How will we know when it's over?"

"Oh, you'll know."

"And how will we know if it's worked?"

"Find your friend," the woman replied. "If she's still possessed, it didn't work. If she's back to normal, it did."

Grace sighed, slid the plastic bowl of purple gunk across the table, and picked it up. She wrinkled her nose at the pungent smell.

"What's in that stuff?" asked Adie.

"Oh, lots of things," said Mrs. Quinlan. "Herbs and soils, insects and fish parts, a little excrement, a frog's heart, some eggshell—"

"Where did you get a frog's heart?"

"From a walrus. Twit."

The old woman gathered the smaller potions together and placed them in a large tweed bag.

"Now, take good care of these brews," she warned. "And if you're not using it until Monday, keep the purple stuff in the fridge."

"My mom's going to love that," muttered Grace.

✳✳✳

Monday lunchtime was the only conceivable time that the girls could perform the incantation. They needed to ensure that the non-Una would be in the building, that teachers and students would not be coming in and out of classrooms, and that they would have time to complete the process without missing any classes and bringing attention to their activities. Luckily, being the newest, farthest away part of the school, the P block had not yet become a popular haunt for any regular groups during the lunch hour. With any luck, the girls wouldn't be disturbed.

"Ugh!" Jenny exclaimed, as Grace pulled the lid off the bowl of congealed purple gloop. "That smells even worse than it did on Friday. Did you keep it in the fridge, like Old Cat Lady said?"

"Yes, I did," snapped Grace, reeling from the stench herself. "And my mom wasn't too impressed. I had to tell her it was for a science experiment. Not sure she believed me."

"Do we really have to spread that stuff all over our faces?"

"Yes," Grace replied firmly. "We're going to do exactly what Mrs. Quinlan said. This needs to work. And try not to drip it onto the floor."

"Who's worried about getting in trouble with the janitor when we've got a potential bunch of demons on our hands?" said Jenny.

"I'm worried. We don't need anybody asking questions about this stuff."

"Right," said Rachel, stooping tenderly down to

kneel on her uninjured leg and marking the carpet with a piece of chalk. "Here's where we all have to stand. Grace, you're at the top there. Adie, you're opposite her and Jenny's opposite me. Everyone ready to go?"

The others nodded in unison, then reluctantly scooped up handfuls of the purple goo and began smearing it over their faces.

"I think I'm going to be sick!" Adie retched.

"Breathe through your mouth," Grace mumbled, trying desperately not to inhale the stench, "and careful not to get it in your eyes."

Standing on their markers, they looked at each other with apprehension.

"I'd just like to point out," said Jenny, holding her purple-stained hands out in front of her, "how completely ridiculous we look." No one argued. "I just hope that crazy Old Cat Lady isn't playing us for a bunch of fools."

"Me too," said Grace, "because if she is, we can say good-bye to Una forever."

"Not to mention the Beast," said Adie.

"Let's get started then," Rachel interjected. "Grace?"

Grace took out a crumpled piece of paper with Mrs. Quinlan's scribbled verse and cleared her throat.

"We stand above an open portal,
Linking demon realm and mortal,
East and West and North and South,
Will alter, now, this hellish mouth.
Take back our uninvited guest,
And rid us of this wicked pest,
What's yours is yours, call back your kind,
And grant to us our peace of mind."

Deep in the ground, far beneath their feet, a low rumbling began. The sound grew and grew, and soon they could feel the vibrations tingling through their bodies. Small drops of foul-smelling purple gunk dripped from their faces and hands as the floor trembled underneath them.

"Does this mean it's working?" whispered Adie.

"Shh!" Grace hissed. "Keep your eyes open!"

They held their positions around the well, keeping their eyes peeled for any hint of unwanted visitors. The trembling continued until there was a sudden and violent movement in the air. The floor didn't budge, but the girls felt a rapid drop, like they were flying down the track of a giant roller coaster. They struggled to stay on their feet and fought back the urge to be sick as the motion, coupled with the fetid stench of the potion, turned their stomachs. Everything began to shift from side to side then, forcing the girls to grab on to one another to keep from falling. Rachel flinched in pain, leaning heavily on Adie's arm.

"I can't stay standing!" she yelled. "Grace!"

"Just hold on!" Grace shouted, squeezing her eyes shut against the overpowering nausea.

"No!" Adie screamed. "It's…it's one of *them*!"

Grace opened her eyes. Adie was staring, terrified, at the center of their circle. A thin, dark swirl of mist curled up from the floor, formed a handlike shape, and gripped the carpet with its claws. A second hand grabbed on, dragging up a pair of shoulders, like a fallen climber hauling himself over the edge of a cliff.

"Jenny! The little bags!" shouted Grace.

Jenny let go of Grace and rummaged in her pockets. Pulling out one of the cloth bags, she held the ties in both hands.

"Watch your feet!" Adie shrieked.

Jenny looked down just in time to see the demon lunge for her ankle. She fell over backward, kicking her feet into the air and smacking onto the ground hard enough to make her teeth rattle in her head. The bag slid across the floor, finally stopping near the exit.

"Get another one," Grace cried. "Quick!"

Jenny snatched another bag from her pocket and sat up, with her head still spinning, gripping the ties in both hands. Leaning forward, she wrenched the ties apart and shut her eyes against the falling powder. The others watched the fine dust settle over the demon, now visible up to the waist. It opened its mouth in a silent scream as the particles landed on it in tiny burning fires. They dissolved the shrieking creature until nothing remained but a small dark patch on the carpet. Meanwhile, the deep underground rumbling continued.

"It's not over yet!" Grace gasped, grabbing hold of Jenny's arm as she rejoined the circle. "Keep watching, everyone!"

Jenny's lip trembled as she spotted another gathering of dark mist in the same spot.

"There!" She pointed, already fishing another bag out of her pocket.

Yanking the ties apart, she looked down to watch the dust settle, but the demon was too fast. It lashed out with its misty hand, snatching Rachel's ankle. The dark powder singed its surface, but then rolled uselessly down its back. Jenny gazed in horror as the creature dragged itself out of the floor and pushed its face into Rachel's shin. Little by little, it disappeared and Rachel's eyes turned a deep, luminous shade of green.

"Rach!" Grace screamed.

"Come on! We only have a minute!" Jenny cried, propelling the others into action.

Grace raced behind Rachel and looped her arms into her friend's, pinning them behind her back. Jenny fell to her knees, throwing her arms around Rachel's legs and holding on tight. Adie pulled out a porcelain cup just as Rachel began to struggle.

"*Now!*" said Jenny.

Adie smashed the cup on the ground, said *exitus, exitus, exitus*, and ducked down to grab hold of Rachel's waist as the smoke wafted upward. Rachel thrashed powerfully, refusing to breathe. Her head snapped back, hitting Grace in the forehead and sending her crashing into the wall behind them. Adie leaped up, twisting Rachel's arms behind her again, and receiving a painful head-butt in return. Jenny gritted her teeth and held on fast, waiting for the grappling to end. Finally, they heard the sound of Rachel sucking in air between her teeth. Within moments the struggle was over. Grace crawled forward and looked into Rachel's eyes.

"She's fine," she said, trying not to aggravate the pain splitting her skull. "You can let go."

Rachel dropped to the floor, crying out as the pain

crunched through her sprained knee. Jenny draped a comforting arm over her, keeping one hand on the floor to monitor the sound beneath.

"I think it's dying down," she said.

The others listened carefully as the sound retreated, going deeper and deeper. Suddenly, there was a piercing flash of light that sent them sprawling across the floor. Then silence.

"What in God's name is *going on* in here?!"

The girls blinked and squinted at the figure holding open the double doors. As their eyes recovered from the glaring flash, they could see Mrs. Hennelly in the P block exit, surrounded by students, and looking fiercely annoyed.

"Um," said Grace, her words a little slurred. "Science experiment?"

chapter 12
the french connection

"What is that *smell*?"

"What's all over their faces?"

"It's poo!"

"It's not poo. It smells worse than poo."

Grace wiped her face with her sleeve, keeping her head down as she and her friends passed the humiliating guard of honor that had formed along the corridor. Tittering laughter reverberated around the hall as Mrs. Hennelly led the unfortunate group of girls to Principal Evans's office.

"Don't you all have classes to go to?!" the teacher shrieked, causing the jeering crowd to slowly disperse.

The girls sat down wearily outside the office and waited to be called in.

"Damage to school property," Mrs. Hennelly muttered, folding her arms, "soiling of your own school uniforms, disrespecting the areas you have been generously given for lunchtimes. I don't know what's come over you girls. *Hmm?* What was going on in there?"

The girls stared quietly ahead and didn't attempt to answer. When the time came, they filed in to the principal's office and stood politely in a straight line. Principal Evans and Vice Principal Collins sat behind a long table, looking perplexed by the four purple-stained faces staring back at them. Nobody spoke for a long minute.

"I guess I have to ask," sighed Mr. Collins. "What were you girls doing in the P block that resulted in a stained and scorched carpet, a stench that apparently resists even the strongest air fresheners, and a number of minor injuries to yourselves?"

Grace opened her mouth to speak but, unable to think of anything to say, shut it again.

"This is a very serious matter, girls," Mrs. Evans said, unimpressed by their silence. "We will be contacting your parents, and I expect an explanation before the day is out."

Nodding curtly to Mr. Collins, she gave the girls one last severe look, wrinkled her nose at the appalling smell, and left. Mr. Collins slumped his shoulders and sighed again.

"This is the second time you all have caused a commotion in recent days. Are you going to give me any explanation? Did this have anything to do with Tracy Murphy?"

Grace jumped at the opportunity.

"Yes, sir. Sorry, sir. We were going to put this smelly stuff in Tracy's locker and...well, there was a bag of it and..."

"I left my glasses sitting on the bag, sir," Jenny cut in, "right under the window. And the sun was shining in, through the glasses, and it burned the carpet, sir."

"I've never seen you wear glasses, Jenny," Mr. Collins said.

"They're ugly, sir. I never wear them. Mom makes me bring them to school, though."

"Is that right? Go on."

"The carpet must've been smoldering really close to the bag, sir," Grace continued, getting into the swing of things now. "And the stuff got warm. And when we picked it up, it burst."

"It was so loud." Rachel nodded. "We all got scared and fell back."

"I hit my head, sir," said Adie.

"And the smelly stuff went everywhere," said Grace.

"I hit my head, sir," repeated Adie, slightly louder.

"I heard you, Adie. Are you all all right? Should I be arranging a ride to the hospital for any of you?"

"No, no," Grace said, trying to smile. "We're fine. We just got scared, sir."

"Well," said Mr. Collins, raising his eyebrows, "that's *some sort* of explanation, I suppose."

"Glad we could clear that up, sir," said Grace, turning to leave with the others.

"Where do you think you're all going?"

The girls turned back to the vice principal with confused faces.

"You brought in some vile-smelling substance to defile another student's locker," he said, leaning forward. "This disgusting prank went awry, and you ended up defiling an entire school block. Did you think that with that bizarre, and frankly questionable, explanation, you were off the hook?"

"Oh. No, sir," Grace replied, looking down at her shoes.

"Detention," he said firmly. "Every lunchtime for two weeks."

The girls gawked.

"And you're going to help the janitor clean up that mess," Mr. Collins went on.

"Yes, sir," the girls chorused in monotone.

"You're dismissed," he said. "And I don't want to see any of you in this office again!"

✳ ✳ ✳

After many minutes of scrubbing with endless wads of tissue paper, the girls emerged from the bathroom.

"*Two weeks* of detention!" said Rachel.

"At least it's just at lunchtime," sighed Grace. "He could have made us do after-school detention."

"I guess so. But still."

"Hey!" said Adie, shaking Grace's sleeve. "There's Una! Hey, *Una!*"

Una swerved through the student traffic and made her way over to them, smiling. Adie rushed forward and hugged her.

"How are you? Are you okay?"

"I'm fine, Adie. Thank you."

Adie stepped back to look at her uncertainly, as if waiting for the punch line. Grace frowned.

"We were worried about you, Una. How are you?" she said.

"I'm fine, Grace. Thank you. But I think you should stop."

"Sorry?"

She stepped forward and stared into Grace's eyes.

"I mean it," she said in a low, threatening tone. "Stop."

Grace felt a chill wash over her like she'd never experienced before. She dropped her eyes.

"But now I'm late for class," the non-Una beamed, suddenly cheerful again. "You should hurry too."

The girls sadly watched the creature that used to be their friend hurry to class. All that trouble, all that danger, and the incantation hadn't worked. And it was obvious the demon inhabiting Una's body had had enough of their exorcising efforts.

✳✳✳

Grace scraped at the purple remains of Mrs. Quinlan's potion on her wrist and sighed heavily. She was usually the most conscientious student in her group of friends, but even she was ignoring Ms. Lemon's recitation of the French irregular verbs.

"Mrs. Vander Tramp," Ms. Lemon called to the class. "Now repeat each verb as I point to the relevant letter. For *M*, *Monter*, for *R*, *Rester*, and so on...

Grace, Adie, Jenny! Are you three paying attention, or is something on your desks more interesting?"

"Sorry, Miss," the girls droned. They reluctantly raised their eyes to the board and repeated the verbs with the rest of the class.

"Excellent," said Ms. Lemon, rubbing the name off the whiteboard. "Now, I want all of you to write down all fourteen verbs without my help."

The class groaned as one and opened their notebooks.

"So what now?" Adie whispered, slowly coloring in a corner of her notebook with a blue pen.

"I don't know," replied Grace, staring at the row of feet under the next table. "I just don't know."

"I didn't think it would be that hard," Jenny sniffed. "I don't want to have to do that again."

"I don't think there'd be much point in doing that again," Grace murmured. "I mean, it obviously didn't work."

"I miss Una." Adie's voice cracked as she gently laid her pen on the desk.

Grace took a deep breath, holding back the tears

that were welling up inside her. She missed her friend too. As each disastrous enchantment failed, it felt like they were getting further and further away from Una, and closer and closer to the evil of the power they'd unleashed. She thought of their first spell and tried to imagine what Tracy Murphy's last moments would feel like. Would she see it coming? Would it hurt? Grace tried to remember if the Beast had any brothers or sisters. Probably not. They'd undoubtedly have equally fierce reputations around school if they did exist. But there *was* a Mrs. Murphy, mother of the Beast, unpleasant though she was. And probably a Mr. Murphy too. Someone was going to miss her.

"Do you think she's still in there?" Adie said softly.

"Huh?"

"Our Una. Is she just jammed down inside herself, underneath that demon? Do you think she knows what's going on? Do you think she's scared?"

Grace shook her head.

"I don't know."

"I hope she's just asleep or something." Adie traced

an old scar on the school desk with her finger. "I hope she's not awake in the dark, all alone."

Grace tried to imagine what being trapped inside herself would feel like. She hoped the real Una was asleep too.

"Are you three waiting for a special invitation before you join this class?"

Ms. Lemon's sharp tone snapped Grace out of her dark thoughts, but not Adie.

"Sorry, Miss," Grace said quietly, knuckling down to work.

"Adie?" Ms. Lemon said, raising one eyebrow.

Adie was too deep in thought to hear. Jenny nudged her gently.

"*What?*" Adie barked.

"I *said,*" replied Ms. Lemon, her voice rising angrily as she walked toward Adie's desk, "are you waiting for a special invitation? Or would you like to sit outside the room for the duration of the class?"

"Sorry," Adie huffed, reaching to pick up her pen but accidentally flicking it under the table in front.

"*Excusez-moi?*" Ms. Lemon's cheeks flushed with anger.

"*J'ai dit que je suis désolée!*" Adie starting sobbing, as though dropping her pen was the last straw on such a horrible day. "*Je n'ai pas de l'intention d'être difficile, mais je suis si fatiguée. Je veux être chez moi!*"

The whole class put down their pens and turned to look at her in amazement.

"What did you say?" the teacher asked quietly.

"*Comment?*" Adie asked, looking up with a tearstained face. "*J'ai dit que je suis fatiguée. J'ai besoin d'un bain, mais je dois rester à l'école. Monsieur Collins est fâché et ce n'est pas notre faute, et*—Ah!"

She stopped suddenly and glared at Jenny, who had given her a swift kick under the table. Her friend stared at her, wide-eyed, trying to silently communicate the problem.

"Oh," Adie said quietly, after a few moments. She said nothing more, but took Grace's pen and started jotting down the irregular verbs, hoping that the teacher would just move on. She didn't.

Ms. Lemon stared at her, then gave the other two a strange look.

"You three are to stay behind after class," she said finally. "I want to talk to you."

"Nice going," muttered Grace, as Ms. Lemon walked back to the front of the class.

"I was just saying I was tired," Adie pleaded, "*et Monsieur Collins est fâché et—*"

"*Je t'ai compris!*" Grace hissed, snatching back her pen. "But knock it off! She's looking at us weird now. So is the whole class."

"Sorry. I didn't know I was doing it."

"*Ça c'est le troisième—*" Jenny blinked hard and shook her head. "I mean, that's spell number three: we all become fluent in French. We're down to number three!"

"One more spell," Adie said, the tears falling afresh. "One more, and after that—splat!"

"*Oui,*" moaned Grace, and laid her head down on the desk.

When the class was over, Grace, Adie, and Jenny stood to attention in front of Ms. Lemon's desk.

"You've pulled something out of the well, haven't you?" said Ms. Lemon.

Grace's mouth fell open.

"What?" she croaked.

"Look"—Ms. Lemon shook her head and folded her arms—"if you're dealing with a demon, you don't have time to be coy. Have you pulled something out of the well or haven't you?"

"We have," Jenny replied.

"By accident," Grace leaped in. "We didn't mean to. We were...we were trying out Rachel's new Ouija board and—"

"I knew there was something fishy going on." The teacher leaned back against her desk, sighing as if disappointed with herself. "As soon as I saw that snowstorm, I knew. I should have been more vigilant."

"You know about the well," Adie asked, "and the demons?"

"I do," Ms. Lemon replied, looking stern. "And *you* know how to make a state-altering potion, judging by the smelly mess I saw in the P Block today. And if you know how to do that, how could you be so irresponsible as to plunk a Ouija board over a demon well?"

"We didn't," replied Grace. "I mean, we don't. We didn't know there was a demon well there. We didn't know what a demon well *was*. And we don't know how to a make a…*thingy* potion. We don't know anything about that stuff."

"Then where—?"

Ms. Lemon stopped suddenly and closed her eyes.

"Vera," she said. "Vera Quinlan's helping you."

Grace nodded.

"How was Vera involved in your summoning of a demon?" the teacher asked.

"She wasn't," said Grace. "We asked her for help because we didn't know what to do to stop the spells."

"What spells?"

Grace proceeded to explain how she and her friends had attempted to dabble in witchcraft by casting a list of spells. How they had tried out a real Ouija board in school when the Career Night was happening, and how the demon they had accidentally summoned had possessed their friend and was executing each of their failed spells.

"Well," said Ms. Lemon after a moment. "It could be worse, I suppose. So you all become fluent in French for a while—and then what? You get your favorite lunches at school, or something?"

"Not exactly." Grace looked to the other two, but neither seemed willing to speak. "Our first spell was… we did it right after Jenny got punched by this bully and…you see, Una was really upset and—"

"Spit it out."

"We did a spell to make Tracy Murphy get hit by a bus."

Grace's eyes shot to the floor. She waited for the horribly long silence to end.

"And this is the last of only two spells remaining?" said the teacher.

Grace looked up warily and nodded.

"Right," said Ms. Lemon, taking out a notebook and pen, "then we don't have much time."

"You're not mad?" said Grace.

"Mad?"

"About the spell we did on Tracy Murphy."

"Girls," the teacher said gently, "I was in middle school too, you know. I know how hard it can be. It was an extremely silly, childish thing to do, but I think you're being punished enough for it now."

The girls looked at each other in faint hope.

"Now," said Ms. Lemon, getting down to business, "you've tried the state-altering incantation, which obviously hasn't worked. So I presume you've already tried an exorcism enchantment, which also didn't work."

"Yeah," replied Jenny. "That was a total disaster. Una went crazy and totally wrecked the A block trying to chase us down."

Adie and Grace shot her an accusing look.

"So that was you all as well?" said the woman. "Wonderful. It sounds like we'll have to be wary of Una. If that demon has resisted being pulled out *and* being sucked back down the well, then it's a strong one. We don't want to anger it any more than necessary."

"So you can help us?" Adie asked.

"I can try."

"Great!" exclaimed Jenny. "Then we don't need Old Cat Lady anymore."

"Not exactly," said Ms. Lemon. "I'm going with you to Vera's house after school. You need all the help you can get."

chapter 13
a wiccan reunion

"So how do you know Mrs. Quinlan?" Rachel was still trying to catch up on what she'd missed. In the space of one afternoon, the others had managed to recruit another adult who not only knew all about the demon well, but was going to help them get Una back.

"Oh, it was a very long time ago," replied Ms. Lemon, lifting her feet as she walked, trying to avoid the early evening dew already settling on the football field. "We both had an interest in the occult, just like you girls, and it kind of brought us together."

"You were good friends?" said Grace.

"The best. Very close."

"But you don't see each other now?"

"We haven't spoken in years," said Ms. Lemon. "We…we had a falling-out."

"A fight?" said Jenny. "Over what?"

Ms. Lemon sighed.

"We just had a difference of opinion, that's all."

Jenny opened her mouth to push the matter further, but Grace silenced her with a look.

A chorus of cat meows erupted as they walked up the driveway of the house in Wilton Place, so loud that it must have alerted Mrs. Quinlan. She was already pulling the door open as the girls stepped onto the porch.

"What have I done to be forever plagued by your faces?!" she snapped as a welcome. "Why didn't it work? What did you do wrong?"

"We didn't do anything wrong, Mrs. Quinlan," Grace replied. "It just didn't work."

"Lies."

"It's true," said Ms. Lemon, stepping last into the porch light. "It seems they carried out the incantation as instructed. The demon was too powerful."

Mrs. Quinlan stepped back as if she'd been struck. Her eyes went wide with surprise, then narrowed to slits.

"Beth," she said quietly. "Long time, no see."

"How've you been, Vera?"

"Can't complain."

"You're…you're looking well."

"Right back at ya."

"May I come in?"

Mrs. Quinlan wriggled her jaw from side to side, as if chewing on a sweet.

"S'pose," she muttered. She turned and stamped back to the kitchen.

"The girls have been filling me in on the situation," said Ms. Lemon as she and the girls followed closely behind. "We're in quite a lot of trouble here."

"*They're* in quite a lot of trouble," Mrs. Quinlan corrected her. "*I* didn't summon any demon."

"No," said Ms. Lemon, "but we can't expect the children to fix this alone. I know you agree with me, or you wouldn't have done so much to help them already."

"Didn't do much," Mrs. Quinlan waved a hand dismissively, "and it doesn't matter anyway, because whatever I tell them to do hasn't been working."

Ms. Lemon sat down at the table and smiled at her old friend. Grace watched Mrs. Quinlan's eyes boring into the French teacher. She looked like a boxer eyeing up her opponent before a fight.

"I feel so old now," said Ms. Lemon, still smiling, "sitting with you after all these years. We were so young back then, so innocent."

Mrs. Quinlan sat in silence, picking at a knot in the wood of the table with her fingernail.

"They remind me of us," Ms. Lemon went on. "When they told me their story, our school days just came flooding back to me."

"You were in school together?" asked Rachel.

"In Saint John's." Ms. Lemon nodded.

"You two are the same *age*?" Jenny blurted out.

Mrs. Quinlan shot her a fiery look.

"Yes, we're the same *age*."

"We had our own little coven," said Ms. Lemon, a

smile still playing on her lips as she remembered, "like you girls, but there were only three of us. Us two and Meredith. We were thick as thieves, determined to become great witches. But then, of course, we discovered the demon well."

"And we found out the hard way that the occult is not all fun and games," said Mrs. Quinlan grimly.

"Why'd you stop talking to each other?" Jenny asked.

"Jenny!" Grace chided her.

"What? They're talking about it anyway. I want to know."

Ms. Lemon looked at Mrs. Quinlan, waiting for her to answer. But no answer came.

"By the time we were old enough to leave school," Ms. Lemon said, "we had vowed to do all we could to keep the town safe from the demon well. Only, we had different ideas about what that meant."

"*I* believed," Mrs. Quinlan cut in, "that in order for people to be safe, they should know as much as possible about it. I felt it was necessary to inform the town of the *presence* of the demon well, and that way they would know to stay away from it. *She* thought we should keep it a secret."

"It was the only way," said the teacher.

"*How* can people be safe from a danger they don't know is *there*?" said Mrs. Quinlan.

"I came back to the school," replied Ms. Lemon, "to watch over the well."

"Lot of good that did."

"Yes," sighed Ms. Lemon, "I wasn't vigilant enough, and these girls are paying the price. But your way didn't work either, Vera."

"Did you tell people about the well?" asked Grace.

"I told them about it." Mrs. Quinlan nodded. "Decades ago. Everyone said I was crazy. The whole town just laughed at me."

"I was so sorry about that," Ms. Lemon said sincerely. "I wanted to talk to you so many times over the years. After your husband left town, I was so close to coming to this house. But I never did."

"Did your husband leave because he thought you were nuts too?" asked Jenny.

"No," Mrs. Quinlan snapped. "For your information, Miss Nosey Parker, he hated *cats*. He said to me one day, 'Get rid of the cats or I'm moving to South America.' 'Don't forget your toothbrush,' I said."

"What about the third one in your coven?" said Grace. "Where is she?"

"Meredith? She…" Ms. Lemon paused as the two women exchanged meaningful glances. "She left. We never heard from her again."

"Moved to Romania or someplace," Mrs. Quinlan grunted. "Good riddance."

"So she won't be helping us too, then?" Jenny asked.

"No. You're stuck with just the two of us. More than you deserve, if you ask me," the Old Cat Lady snarled.

"So what spell or incantation thingy are we going to try next?" asked Grace.

Ms. Lemon took a deep breath and looked at each of the girls.

"The only option left to us is one you would hope never to have to perform. It's extremely dangerous and will require each of you to be very brave."

"More demons?" Adie frowned.

"No, you're going to focus on just Una for this one. But first you must collect the necessary…buffers."

"Buffers?" said Grace.

"Something to cushion you from the force that has possessed your friend," said the teacher. "This creature has resisted some very powerful magic, and the only tactic we have left is to curse the demon permanently. Bind it so it is hurled back down the well and can never again return."

"Will this one definitely work?" asked Jenny.

"If it is performed correctly, almost certainly."

"Great!"

"Don't celebrate too soon," said Ms. Lemon. "You have to gather the required…*materials*, first."

"Which are?" asked Grace. The women exchanged glances.

"Trapped souls," Mrs. Quinlan replied. "Listen. When spirits fail to reach the afterlife, but cannot return to their living bodies, they become trapped in a plane that is somewhere between our world and the next. We can sometimes hear them, sometimes see them, but the connection is weak. They cannot see or hear enough of our world to interact properly with it. For them, it drifts in and out like a badly tuned radio. It's an uncomfortable existence, and often prevents them from communicating with each other in any meaningful way. As a result, they experience discomfort and extreme loneliness, which drives them to madness."

"That's awful!" exclaimed Adie. "The poor things."

"Yes, little girl, it is tragic," the woman said flatly, "but there is nothing we living beings can do for them. They, on the other hand, can do us tremendous damage."

"How?"

"You've heard of poltergeists, haunted houses, and other paranormal events?"

"Yes. You mean those things are real?"

"Well, I'm sure some of them," Mrs. Quinlan said, waving her hand, "are just the ramblings of brain-dead idiots, or fools trying to make a few bucks. But these things actually exist. Lost spirits *can* influence objects and people on our plane to a certain extent. Always remember that they are desperate to connect, to *interact* with others in any way possible. If they make you scream with fear, that's an interaction. If they make you bleed by flinging some object at your head, that's an interaction."

"And these are the things," Grace said worriedly, "that we have to *collect*."

"Yep."

"But *how?*"

Ms. Lemon took over in a calm voice, trying to reassure the girls as she spoke.

"Luckily," she said, "these spirits gather together in groups—their desire for company extends to each other, you see—so you can collect the half dozen or so that you need at one time."

"So," asked Jenny, frowning, "we just grab them and shove them in a jar or something?"

"Unfortunately," her teacher replied, "it's a little more complicated than that. The collection can only take place during a full moon, when the link between the two planes is strongest. One—*and only one*—of you will take a chi orb to the gathering and perform the ritual. If all goes to plan, the spirits will be trapped in the orb until you need them."

"Where do we get a *cheee* orb?" said Jenny.

Mrs. Quinlan dug into a heavy cloth bag hanging on a hook by the stove, pulled out what looked like a navy-blue paperweight, and tossed it onto the table. It landed with a loud bang and, oddly, didn't break, bounce, or roll.

"Careful!" Adie squealed, jumping back in fright.

"Relax, Abbey," said Mrs. Quinlan. "It's unbreakable. By us, anyway."

Grace took a deep breath. "Where do we take it?"

"There is a *gathering* nearby," Mrs. Quinlan replied, riffling through a drawer before pulling out a dirty, well-used map and spreading it across the kitchen table. "Here." She pointed.

She looked up after a long silence.

"You're all a little pale," she said.

"No," Adie shivered, stepping back from the table and slowly sitting on a moth-eaten armchair against the wall. "No way."

"The Stone House," Rachel whispered.

"You know this place?" asked Ms. Lemon.

"It's in the field next to Rachel's house," breathed Grace. "We sometimes dare each other to go out to it in the dark. But none of us have ever managed it."

"Una got close that time." Jenny frowned. "She said she heard voices in there."

"It's very probable that she did," Mrs. Quinlan said. "There should be enough spirits in there to make a cacophony under the right moon."

"And one of us has to go in there *alone*?" Adie's olive skin went grayer.

"Yep," the woman sniffed, folding the map and pushing it back into the overflowing drawer. "*Your* mess. *You* fix it."

"What she means, girls," Ms. Lemon cut in diplomatically, "is that because you summoned the demon, you have to be the ones to eject it. We're going to help you as much as we possibly can but, this particular part, you have to do yourselves."

"Like I said," grunted Mrs. Quinlan. "Your mess. You fix it."

✳✳✳

Wednesday night's full moon loomed over them like a horrible nightmare. The girls were in their first lunchtime detention following the purple-stinking-gunk fiasco, and they still had not discussed who would be the one to collect the lost souls. No one had even mentioned the Stone House since they left Mrs. Quinlan's house the previous evening, and time was running out. None of them wanted to volunteer.

"We draw straws," Grace said. "It's the only fair way."

"I can't do it," Adie replied. "I know I'll get the short straw, and I just *can't do it*. I can't go out there alone. I think I'd *die*."

"None of us want to do it," Rachel said softly, "but we have no choice. I agree with Grace. We leave it up to chance."

Jenny nodded solemnly in agreement.

"Shall we do it now?" said Grace. "Get it over and done with?"

She got no reply, so she pulled two pencils out of her case and snapped each of them in two, making sure that one of the broken pieces was much smaller than the others. Closing her fingers around the pieces, she jumbled them behind her back, then held out her fist to the others. Rachel reached out to pick one.

"Wait!" Adie hissed. "Let's do it tomorrow. Please? Right before we've got to go out there. I can't do it otherwise. I can't get through a whole day if I know I have to go out there."

"Fair enough." Grace nodded. "That's probably best, anyway. Throw whoever it is in the deep end. That way they won't have time to get scared."

They carried on with their detention essays, glad of the temporary reprieve, and tried their best not to think about Wednesday night.

"What does Ms. Lemon have us doing after school today?" Jenny asked.

"Picking herbs and weeds, she said," replied Rachel.

"Think I prefer Mrs. Quinlan's way of doing things."

"Doing all that stuff herself, you mean?"

"Yeah, and we just wait for the red scarf," said Jenny.

"I don't mind," whispered Grace. "It'll take our minds off…"

She stopped and sighed heavily in apology for bringing their minds back to the task ahead.

"I'd prefer to be at home watching TV," Jenny muttered.

chapter 14
no strings

The fresh evening air lifted their spirits more than they had expected. It felt like they were on a field trip, strolling through the woods near the school, scrounging for weeds and mushrooms on the damp, muddy ground. They competed against each other, racing to find a herb or wildflower described in Ms. Lemon's encyclopedia, then protesting loudly when their teacher shook her head, smiling, and explained why it was the wrong species. In all the time they'd spent in and around the school, they had no idea the area was home to so many different plants and animals. Each tree was like a little ecosystem sheltering dozens of weeds, fungi, and tiny life-forms.

"Ugh!" exclaimed Rachel, pointing to a collection of orange blobs growing out of the bark of a tall willow. "They look like little aliens, sucking the life out of the tree."

"Very well spotted, Rachel," Ms. Lemon applauded. "*Dimerella lutea*. And it's on our list."

Rachel nodded solemnly.

"I thought so," she lied.

"You're doing great, girls! Just one ingredient left—*Pertusaria hymenea*. It looks a little like a gray-white splash of paint on a tree, with tiny dark discs sitting on top. Yell when you see it."

The girls scrambled around the woods, giggling and squealing as they pushed each other out of the way to win the final round.

"Got it!" Adie yelled.

The others groaned in defeat as she jumped up and down, pointing upward at the pale-colored lichen stuck fast to the trunk of a horse chestnut tree.

"You've got eagle eyes, Adie," Ms. Lemon said with a smile. "Ah, now that's up a little high. Someone will have to do a little climbing."

"I'm on it," chirped Jenny, already gripping the bark with her fingertips and securing one foot in a knot.

"Take it easy," her teacher urged. "Don't rush now."

Pieces of scraped-off bark fell to the ground as Jenny, her tongue stuck out one side of her mouth in concentration, steadily edged upward. Ms. Lemon's brow furrowed as she looked at the girl's unsuitable school shoes. She opened her mouth—and Jenny slipped.

The others gasped, racing forward as Jenny slipped again. Her mouth opened in a scream as she toppled in slow motion out of the tree and toward the ground.

Only, she never hit the ground.

Instead the girls watched, stunned, as Jenny floated horizontally, her eyes squeezed shut, about hip-height off the weed-covered soil. Slowly, she opened her eyes.

"Whooaa!" she shrieked, punching the air. "Awesome!"

Grinning widely, Jenny craned her neck to look

at the others. Grace circled her friend slowly, waving her hands above her and below her, as she'd seen magicians do to show there were no strings attached. Nope, no strings. It was spell number two, all right.

"Are you stuck?" she said. "I mean, can you move around?"

"Think so," said Jenny. "Watch this!"

"Maybe you should—" Ms. Lemon started before a loud whoop of joy cut her off.

Jenny threw her head back, sending herself into a backward somersault, flying higher and higher into the air. The others cheered and clapped, then tried to get themselves airborne. Grace and Adie held hands as they tentatively rose a few inches off the ground and hovered unsteadily, smiling with glee. Rachel, not to be outdone by Jenny, bent her knees, ignoring the pain that still shot through her right leg, and jumped as high as she could, soaring into the air at full speed. Leaves and small twigs brushed her face as she swept upward into the sky.

"Rachel!" Ms. Lemon shouted. "Get back down here this *instant*!"

"It's just spell number two, Miss," Adie said. "The one where we can fly!"

"I got that much, Adie, thank you," said the teacher, "but that doesn't mean it's not dangerous."

She gave them all stern looks as Rachel and Jenny swooped down to join Adie and Grace in hovering just off the woodland floor.

"I realize this seems like just a little fun," said Ms. Lemon carefully, "but you have no idea how long the spell will last. It could stop working when you're midair. *And* it's very possible someone will see you frolicking around in the sky."

"But, Miss," Rachel moaned, "this is the coolest thing *ever*."

"Yeah." Jenny nodded. "You can't expect us to not even try it out."

Ms. Lemon sighed.

"Oh, all right," she said, "you can fly a little around here. But don't go up too high, in case it wears off, and when we leave the woods, *that's it*. When we're back on the road, your flying's done. Is that clear?"

The girls cheered in unison and took off in various directions, whooping as the wind swept through their hair and made their school ties flutter like wind socks at the airport.

"How do you stay *upright*?" Adie called, her curly locks dangling toward the ground as she struggled to right herself.

"Just think of your feet being heavy," Jenny sang back, "and you'll flip up the right way."

"I can't do it! Am I the only one?"

"Nope," yelled Grace, tipping her foot off a branch in an attempt to swing her head and shoulders upward, "I keep falling over too. Ms. Lemon! What are we doing wrong?"

"Can't help you there I'm afraid, girls," their teacher called back. "Time's almost up now."

Jenny and Rachel flew even faster, trying to fit in as many somersaults and cartwheels as they possibly could, while the other two grumbled in envy, still trying to get control of their movements.

"I think I've got it!" Adie yelled suddenly. "Grace,

bend your knees a little and tighten up your tummy. You just swing upright!"

Grace gasped with joy as she flipped the right way up and flew in a straight line.

"Awesome!"

"Time's up!" Ms. Lemon shouted. "Down you come."

The girls protested loudly.

"Please, Miss," Grace pleaded, "me and Adie have only just got the hang of it."

"I'm sorry, Grace, but that's it. You girls have to get home, and I've got potions to make. Jenny, grab some of that lichen on your way down."

"Will do, Miss," Jenny replied, circling the tree in a wide spiral as she slowly descended.

Grace and Adie landed heavily on the ground, grumbling again that they hadn't had a real chance at flying. But Ms. Lemon wouldn't budge.

"Safely home, all of you," she said. "And make sure you're all ready for tomorrow."

Grace and Adie trudged along the road.

"That's the first time I've been happy in *ages*," said Adie.

Grace grunted sulkily in agreement, dragging her feet so much that the walk downhill from school seemed even longer than usual. Their after-school adventure had completely taken her mind off the depressing situation she and her friends were in, and now she and Adie were as melancholy as ever. She stopped suddenly and gazed up at the darkening sky.

"Adie."

"Yeah?"

Grace looked at her friend, a big grin spreading across her face.

"Let's fly home."

Adie thought for a moment, then smiled.

"Yeah."

Giggling with delight, they glanced around to make sure no one else was on the street, then launched themselves high into the sky, shrieking silently as the air rushed out of their lungs. They definitely had the hang of it now. Swooping past each other, squealing with happy panic when they got too close, they flipped and tumbled, demonstrating air acrobatics that would make Rachel and Jenny green with envy. Slowing to float up as high as they dared, the twinkling lights of the town below seemed reflected in the sky around them. They spun slowly, taking in a panoramic view of the stars, until they felt dizzy, then gently glided downward like feathers on the wind.

"The town looks so pretty from up here," said Adie. "The traffic looks like little rows of fireflies."

"Yeah," Grace said breathlessly. "Wish we could fly forever."

They coasted down, feeling invisible in the air as they could just make out little figures walking on the streets.

"No way!" Adie exclaimed. "That's Trish and Bev! Servants of the Beast."

"But without the Beast." Grace winked.

They smiled wickedly at each other, then dived as one, racing past the two bullies so fast they appeared like school uniform–colored blurs in the atmosphere.

"What the hell was *that*?" Bev squawked.

The maroon blurs rushed past them again, creating gusts of wind that swept their lacquered hair up into ridiculous-looking and uncomfortable hairdos.

"Ghosts!" Trish screeched. "It's *ghosts*! Run!"

She took off at full speed, plowing over Bev in her hurry to get away. Her friend scrambled to her feet and followed suit. Grace and Adie chuckled quietly to themselves as they hung in the air, just out of sight, above the roof of a small shop.

"Look at them go."

"I don't think I've ever seen those two run before," said Adie, grinning widely.

"We should get home, I suppose."

"Guess so. I don't—ah!"

Adie jerked suddenly, dropping a few feet, then rising again.

"Oops, do you think it's—aahh!"

She plummeted suddenly to the roof below, landing on the gable, then sliding off on one side, desperately trying to grip the glossy roof tiles.

"Adie!" Grace screamed. "Hold on!"

But Grace was losing power herself. Dropping quickly, she tried to grip a nearby telephone pole but only managed to catch her fingernails painfully before plunging to the roof below. She smacked onto the dark tiles, sliding swiftly downward. Her feet flew off the edge and her hands scrambled wildly over her head, just managing to grip the gutter before she flew off the roof entirely. With her feet dangling over the concrete below, she squeezed her eyes shut and tried not to think of the growing pain in her hands as her muscles began to cramp.

"Grace!"

Grace could hear Adie's scuttling feet as she struggled to keep her purchase on the slanted roof.

"I'm here, Adie, but I can't hold on much longer!"

"I'm coming!"

The grating sound of Adie's shoes on the tiles got louder as she dragged herself closer to her friend. Grace saw the curly dark locks appear over the edge of the roof.

"Grab my hand," Adie said urgently, securing one foot in the gutter and leaning down as far as she could.

"I can't! I'll fall!"

"I won't let you fall. I promise."

Grace held her breath and, with enormous effort, gripped the gutter tighter with her right hand and reached out with her left. Adie grasped her wrist firmly and pulled her upward. There was a sudden metallic groan, and the gutter broke away from one of its fixtures. The girls screamed in panic, but Adie held fast to her friend as another fixture snapped, then another. Adie was slipping closer to the edge as her foot traveled off the edge with the gutter.

"You're going to fall!" Grace shouted. "Let me go!"

Adie ignored her and, with one last grunting effort, dragged Grace onto the roof just as the gutter detached completely and spun off toward the drainpipe at the side of the building. The girls lay flat against the roof tiles, not daring to move, panting loudly with exhaustion and relief. Grace turned her head slowly to look at Adie, her eyes filling with tears.

"Thanks."

"No worries," Adie wheezed. "So how are we going to get down?"

Glancing around, moving as little as possible, Grace nodded toward one side of the roof.

"Drainpipe."

Clambering down the damp, narrow drainpipe seemed to take forever. After the freedom and grace of being able to fly, they suddenly felt impossibly awkward and heavy. When they finally reached the ground, their legs were like jelly, and the walk home seemed much, much longer than ever before.

***

It felt like forever before Grace finally reached her house and opened her front door.

"Grace? Is that you, love?" Grace's mother's voice was concerned.

"Yeah, Mom."

Grace pulled her key out of the lock and stood for

moment in the light of the hall before going into the warm kitchen.

"You're very late home, sweetheart."

"I know. Sorry. We were collecting some stuff for science class tomorrow."

"What sort of stuff?"

"Just plants and stuff, from around the school."

"Oh. Well, you're just in time for dinner, so wash your hands and sit down at the table."

Grace smiled weakly at her mother as she turned on the cold tap at the kitchen sink and rubbed her hands slowly under the freezing water.

"You look a little tired," her mother said as she tipped some freshly steamed carrots onto two waiting plates. "Are you all right?"

Grace turned off the tap and turned toward the table, drying her hands on a tea towel as she went.

"Yeah," she whispered. "I'm fine."

Her mom's pork chops were not her favorite, but she ate them gladly, somehow feeling comforted by the warm dinner made lovingly for her.

"I'm going to see your aunt Janet on Sunday," her mother said. "She finally got to bring the brand-new puppy home—a little cocker spaniel. He's gorgeous! Why don't you come over with me?"

"I don't know," Grace mumbled. "If I can."

"I thought you were dying to see him," her mother said with surprise. "When I showed you that photo of all the puppies, you didn't shut up about them for the whole day. Don't you want to meet the little guy?"

"Yeah." Grace sighed, stuffing another chunk of pork chop into her mouth. "Just might be busy with the girls, that's all. Sorry, Mom. I do want to see him though. Just maybe not this weekend."

There was a pause, then Grace's mother reached over and stroked the back of Grace's hand.

"Are you sure you're all right, sweetheart?"

Grace looked up and managed a pained smile.

"Yeah, I'm fine."

chapter 15
the stone house

Beneath the deep dark blue of the night sky, sat the heavy silhouette of the Stone House. Even in the light of the full moon, the house was pitch black, like it sucked all the light out of its surroundings. There was no wind, no sound in the air at all. Huddled on Rachel's windowsill, the girls gazed mournfully out at the dreaded shape at the end of the field. Jenny held four matchsticks tightly in her fist. One by one, the girls picked. Grace exhaled loudly as she drew out one of the longer sticks. Rachel did the same. Jenny and Adie exchanged worried looks as Adie reached forward and plucked out a matchstick. She stared hard at the stubby piece of wood between her fingertips, and her bottom lip trembled.

"Sorry, Adie," Jenny whispered, opening her hand to reveal the final stick.

Adie said nothing, but the tears were already dripping down her cheeks and onto the carpet. The others placed the chi orb and a wooden shaker, full of some powder made by Ms. Lemon, into her hands. They moved silently, without speaking, as if the slightest noise would somehow break their friend. Sniffing softly, Adie got to her feet. She turned to give one agonized look to her friends, then disappeared through the bedroom door.

Within moments they could see her in the garden, climbing over the fence. Grace felt a horrible pang in her chest as Adie walked slowly forward. Pausing now and then, Grace could see her shoulders shudder violently and knew that her friend was sobbing with fear. She felt hot tears run down her own face as she remembered Adie's grip on her wrist, pulling her to safety on the roof earlier. Before she knew it, she was on her feet and racing down the field toward the pale figure in the dark.

"Adie, stop!"

Adie swung around.

"Grace, what are you doing? I have to go in *alone*."

Grace grabbed the orb and the wooden shaker, and pushed her friend back toward Rachel's house.

"I'm going in," she said firmly, raising a finger as Adie began to protest. "I've decided, so don't bother arguing with me. I'm going in."

Adie's tears began to fall afresh. She shook her head and hugged Grace tightly.

"Be careful," she whispered.

Grace pulled back and smiled at her.

"See you in a little bit. Don't let the others finish off the marshmallows before I get back."

Adie tried to smile in return as Grace backed away and turned to face the Stone House.

It was only a bungalow, but somehow it seemed to tower over her, its broken gabled roof reaching into the night sky. She heard the soft pad of Adie's feet on the grass get quieter and quieter until they were gone. Squeezing the magical items in her hands, she moved toward the building, close enough now to make out the individual stones in the walls. The roof was mostly gone. It had crumbled away with part of one wall, leaving a gaping hole in one side of the house that revealed nothing but more darkness.

Grace's footsteps seemed too loud. She slowed to a crawl and placed her feet carefully, trying to mute the sound. When she was close enough, she went around the house in a wide circle, until she was facing the front door. A broken, ancient rectangle of wood hung at a slight angle in the doorway. She jerked her head suddenly. Was that a whisper?

Glancing rapidly around, Grace couldn't see anyone. But there it was again. A soft, high-pitched whisper. There was another! And another!

Grace's knees weakened, but she stepped forward. As she got closer to the worm-eaten door, the whispers grew louder and louder. They were discordant and shrill. The sound hurt her ears. Squinting against it, she put her hand on the broken door and pushed. The door swung open, and there was sudden silence.

Grace couldn't see a thing inside the house. It was too dark. Willing herself forward, she felt the grainy stone floor beneath her feet. The moon shone through the dilapidated roof, but it wasn't until she stepped farther inside that she could make out the wooden furniture that lay in pieces around the room. There were no pictures on the walls, and no other evidence that anyone had ever lived in this house. Without warning, the door behind her slammed shut with a loud bang.

Grace let out a small scream and fell to her knees. A loud blast of piercing whispering exploded around her, making her cry out in pain as if her eardrums would burst. Her hands felt numb and useless as she fumbled with the wooden shaker, messily scattering the powder in a circle around herself. Sitting back on her knees again and shutting her eyes against the horrible noise, she cupped the orb in her hands and raised it above her head.

"Time," Ms. Lemon had said. "There's no work involved here, it just takes time. The powder will pull them in eventually."

Grace gripped the heavy blue orb in her hands and desperately wished for it all to be over. The first hit took her totally off guard. Her eyes shot open, and she felt another sharp smack across her face. There was nothing around her but thin air, yet she could swear the strike came from an open hand. She let out a shuddering breath as something behind her pulled at her hair.

Amid the violence, there were gentler attempts at interaction too. She felt something sweep over her arms, like silk being pulled across her skin. But then, *whack*! Another hit.

Grace's eyes were stinging with tears when, below the dreadful hissing whispers, she heard the dull sound of wood dragging over stone. She looked to her left in alarm, just as a chair leg flew at her head. She ducked, barely avoiding it, and struggled with all her strength to keep the orb in both hands. More wooden pieces flew. She managed to avoid two of them, but the third caught her painfully on the shoulder. Warmth trickled down her back, and she knew that she was bleeding.

Tears ran down Grace's face, stinging the cuts on her cheeks. The whispering became shrieking, so loud she was sure the whole town could hear it.

"Please!" she begged aloud. "*Please!*"

She squeezed her eyes shut again—and then the orb gave a powerful shake, heating suddenly until she could barely hold it. Relief flooded through Grace as the shrieking died down to a whisper, and then to silence. She looked up and exhaled softly. It was over.

But wait. Grace squinted. Was that something— something moving in the darkest corner of the room?

"Hello, Grace," said a voice she knew only too well.

✳✳✳

Back in Rachel's room, Jenny had switched off the lights so the girls could see as much as possible through the gloomy darkness outside. Adie sat on her

knees, tucked between the other two, plucking worriedly at her socks as she watched Grace's small frame
disappear into the blackness.

"She's gone in!" Rachel hissed.

"How do you know?" Adie whispered. "Can you
see her?"

"Just about. Before she went inside."

"I can't believe she did it," murmured Jenny.

"What do you think is happening in there?"
asked Adie.

There was a long moment of silence as they each
imagined the worst—screaming ghouls, terrifying
ghosts, and horrible specters wrenching at Grace's
hair, scratching her skin, and pounding on her limbs.

"I can't think about it," Adie's voice rasped in
the dark.

"What's that?" Rachel said, sitting up suddenly.

"What?" said Jenny.

"There, at the back of the field."

"I can't see anything." Jenny was straining her neck
and squinting.

"There!" Rachel pointed urgently. "Something's coming through the ditch."

In the pale light of the moon, they could just make out a dark figure clawing its way through the overgrown brambles to the left of the Stone House. It stood slowly, brushing broken briars from its arms, then raised its face to the sky. Rachel sucked in a panicked breath.

"*It's her!*" she screeched.

✳✳✳

Grace twisted around so quickly, she fell onto her back.

"Una!" she gasped. "Where did you come from?"

"What are you doing here, Grace?" The voice was a chilling monotone.

Grace got clumsily to her feet without using her hands. She held the orb to her stomach, trying to conceal it as best she could.

"The girls dared me to come out here," she said, her voice strained. "Like you did that time, Una. Remember?"

The non-Una had stepped out of the corner and began circling the room, keeping her pulsing red eyes on Grace the whole time. Grace edged toward the doorway.

"I guess we both win the game this time, huh?" she said, trying to smile.

"I know what you're trying to do," said the demon. It took a step forward.

Grace's legs suddenly took flight. She raced through the open door and sprinted toward Rachel's house. She ran so fast she felt sick, but she kept going and did not look back. Behind her, she could hear the pounding of feet. As she got closer to the garden fence, she faltered, squinting against the motion sensor light that suddenly flicked on.

Three figures emerged from the light, urging her on, and reaching out for her.

"She's right behind you, Grace, *run!*" screamed Adie.

But she wasn't quick enough. The non-Una grabbed a handful of her sweater and snapped her back, like a fish caught on a rod. She flew through the air, landing heavily on the ground. She scrabbled at the orb as it rolled away from her fingertips. Suddenly, Grace was flipped onto her back. Helpless, arms pinned by her side, she was now staring straight into the non-Una's terrifying red eyes...

Just when she thought it was all over, Grace felt someone barrel into the demon from behind, sending her flying into the grass. Someone else grabbed Grace's arms and pulled her to her feet.

"The orb!" Grace screamed. "I dropped it!"

"Got it!" she heard Jenny's voice shout in the dark.

Grace reached out for her, clutching Jenny's free hand before making a dash toward the house. She could hear Adie's terror-filled breaths just behind her as she ran. A sudden scream echoed around them.

"*Rachel!*" Jenny shouted. She skidded to a halt, dropped Grace's hand, and raced back the way they had come. Grace and Adie followed, gasping for breath. Again Rachel's frightened cries rang out in the cold air. In the center of the field, she squirmed on her knees as the non-Una held her throat in a powerful grip.

"*Give me the orb!*" the demon's voice growled, its burning red eyes glaring at the heavy paperweight in Jenny's hand.

Jenny stood paralyzed.

"Give me the orb!" it repeated, tightening its grip. Rachel made a painful gurgling sound as she struggled to breathe.

Jenny stepped forward.

"Oh no!" Grace whispered inaudibly, just catching sight of Jenny's left hand as it slipped something out of her pocket.

"Take it." Jenny's lip quivered as she held out the orb.

The red eyes lifted in a horrible smile, and the grip on Rachel's neck loosened. The non-Una reached out to grasp the orb. But just as her fingers touched its smooth surface, Jenny jammed a small cloth bag between her teeth, pulling loose the tie that held it shut, and lunged forward, stuffing the bag into the demon's gaping grin.

The non-Una stumbled backward, spluttering

as the powder escaped down her throat. She wiped frantically at her mouth, coughing huskily as tiny fires burned brightly before rolling off her outstretched tongue. She shook her head, coughing harder as she tried to bring up the teeny flames that had slipped down her throat. Staggering through the grass, she managed one wheezing growl before throwing herself through the briar-filled ditch and disappearing into the night.

The girls didn't waste a second. They turned and fled, their feet pounding on the damp ground as they sprinted back to the house.

They spent the night holding vigil at the window, each of them far too terrified to sleep. It was the longest night of their lives.

chapter 16
out of time

Ms. Lemon and Mrs. Quinlan made a curious pair when waiting together at the school gates. The French teacher stood solemn and still, while her moth-eaten companion made faces at the schoolchildren who pointed and stared, even resorting to sticking out her tongue at a passing busload of unmannerly youngsters.

"You know," she said, sniffing, "might not be so bad to let this bully child get run over. One less smelly teenager in the world wouldn't bother me any."

"You don't mean that, Vera," Ms. Lemon replied evenly as she carefully scanned the gathering crowd. "And there's no point trying to fool me. I know you better than that."

"*Pssh.*"

Mrs. Quinlan sniffed loudly again, casually inspecting the growing mass of noisy students.

"There they are," said Ms. Lemon.

The four girls approaching them looked haggard well beyond their years. Their sunken eyes were sticky with tiredness, and they huddled close together, warily glancing left and right as they reached the gates.

"Whatever we're going to do, we have to do it now," Grace said.

She pulled the orb from her schoolbag and held it out, hoping that one of the women would take it.

"The non-Una's after us."

"She turned up at the Stone House." Jenny took the orb and planted it firmly in Ms. Lemon's hands. "She nearly killed Rachel."

Ms. Lemon looked into the orb, then picking up one end of the scarf around her neck, began to polish it gently.

"You're all very brave," she said, "and we need you to be brave just a little longer."

"We can't!" Adie exclaimed. "You didn't see her. *It*! It's going to kill us!"

Ms. Lemon took Grace's hand and placed the orb back in her palm, closing her fingers around it.

"You've dealt with the consequences of each of your spells," the teacher continued softly. "You found Vera when you needed help. You've taken on demons and defeated them and collected an orb full of wild spirits. You've done things even the most experienced witches have never managed. I'm very proud of you all. *We're* very proud."

She nodded to Mrs. Quinlan, who just curled her lip in reply.

"And you have one task left," said Ms. Lemon.

Mrs. Quinlan pulled out two coils of thin rope from the folds of her clothes.

"These have been soaked in several carefully prepared infusions," she said, holding them out. "Loop them around the demon's wrists and hold on tight. They'll help cement it to the spot."

Rachel and Jenny took one each and pushed them into their jacket pockets.

"This very simple verse is all you need." Ms. Lemon handed Grace a small rolled-up piece of paper and patted her hand gently. "Whisper it into the orb and let it go."

Grace took the verse and nodded slowly.

"Right," Mrs. Quinlan said firmly, "my part's done. I'm out of here. Best of luck, and all that."

"I'll stay in the school until this is all over," Ms. Lemon said quickly, noting their dismal faces. "Just keep reminding yourselves why you're doing this."

"We don't want Tracy Murphy to get killed." Grace sighed. "And—"

"We want Una back," Adie finished.

Ms. Lemon smiled.

"Girls, you know what to do. Go get her."

✳✳✳

Hours later, Grace sat on a table in their lunchroom, turning the blue orb carefully in her hands. Rachel stood by the window biting her nails, while Jenny rolled M&Ms off a desk and into a wastepaper basket waiting underneath. Adie sat with her head in her hands.

They hadn't been able to find the non-Una. They'd looked everywhere, and it was the one problem they hadn't foreseen. They couldn't think of anything else to do now but wait until she showed up.

At least they knew Tracy Murphy was alive and well, thought Grace ruefully, if the heavy tread she could hear in the corridor was anything to go by.

"Is there a party in here or something?"

The Beast strode in, flanked by Trish and Bev, both of whom had made considerable effort with their hairstyles that morning. Bev even posed momentarily at the door to allow the girls a second to appreciate the full effect.

"Hardly," said Grace, tipping the orb into her open bag as discreetly as she could.

"Where's the Freak?" Tracy snapped.

"Don't know," Jenny replied glumly, rolling another candy across the table.

Tracy snatched the wastepaper basket and emptied it angrily over Jenny's head.

"Well," she snarled, tossing the basket into Jenny's lap, "you can tell her *I'm* looking for her!"

"Tell her yourself!" snapped Jenny.

Grace leaped off the table as the Beast grabbed Jenny by the collar and lifted her out of her seat.

"You tell her I'm looking for her! Or else I'll come looking for *you*. Got it?"

"We get it, we get it!" Grace pleaded, catching hold of Jenny as she was plunked back onto her chair. "We'll tell her."

"Good," Tracy sneered. "See you later now."

The henchmen waved and smiled as they followed their leader out of the room.

"I'm sick of her and her stupid cronies!" Jenny shouted, wiping M&Ms and other pieces of garbage from her sweater. "We're jumping through hoops to save her life!"

"I know, I know," Grace soothed.

"Doesn't matter what we're doing if the non-Una

doesn't turn up," said Adie. "Rach, knock that off or you'll make your fingers bleed."

Rachel spat out a bit of a fingernail and clasped her hands in her lap.

"If she doesn't show up soon," she said, "we'll have to go looking for her again."

Scouring the town for an enraged demon was a daunting prospect. If she was hiding from them, she could be anywhere. And they were seriously short on time.

✳✳✳

"Heya, Grace."

Grace fumbled with the lock on her locker door, so stressed she couldn't remember the combination.

"Not now, James." She sighed. "I'm not in the mood."

"Oh. Sorry you're having a bad day. Is there anything I can do?"

"You can go away," she snapped, banging her hand on the metal door before finally remembering her combination and swinging the door open, almost grazing his cheek. She winced. "Sorry."

"That's okay," he said. His crestfallen face broke into a smile. "You can make it up to me by letting me walk you home."

"I'm not walking home. Look, James, I can't deal with this right now. My friend is missing and if I don't find her—"

"Which friend?"

"Una."

"With the short, dark hair? I passed her in the B block a while ago. I'll help you look for her if you like."

"What do you mean? You saw her—today? In *school?*"

"Yeah, before last class. Do you…hey, what's the rush?"

Grace threw the rest of her books into her locker, slammed the door shut, and started running. She reached the corridor and stopped suddenly. Her bag was too light. Swinging it from her shoulder, she emptied the contents onto the floor. A pencil case, a cell phone, an uneaten sandwich wrapped in tinfoil and…nothing else. The orb was gone.

She took off at a run, leaving her belongings scattered on the floor, finally catching up with the others in the main hall.

"She's here," she said, panting. "James saw her at school, in the B block."

"Then let's go," said Jenny.

"Wait!" Grace said, holding her hand up. "The orb. It's gone. *She* must have stolen it."

"What?" Jenny went pale, then took a deep breath. "Okay, we'll have to split up."

"Split up!" Adie squealed. "Are you nuts? We have to stay together!"

"I agree," said Grace. "We need to watch out for each other. She could be anywhere."

"Fine," replied Jenny. "But we need to get our rears in gear if we're going to find her."

"And what then?" said Adie. "She's got the orb, so we can't do Mrs. Quinlan's curse. We're powerless without it."

"Then we have to get it back," Grace said firmly. "Find her, take back the orb, and finish the curse before she gets away."

✷✷✷

Trish and Bev stood huddled outside the school gates as Tracy leaned against the wall beside them and picked her teeth.

"What is it?" said Trish, weighing the blue orb in her hand.

"Don't know," shrugged Bev, "but Grace was looking at it like it was made of gold. Maybe we could sell it or something."

"*I* know what it is—it's a paperweight. For holding down papers. Who'd buy a paperweight?"

"It's not a paperweight," said Bev. "A paperweight's got a flat bottom."

"How do *you* know what a paperweight looks like?" Trish sneered.

"My *mom* has one."

Trish held up the orb to the light. "It's all swirly inside, like it's moving. Freaky."

"Give it here." Bev tried to snatch it from her friend.

"No way! It's mine. Get lost."

"*I* stole it!"

"And then you gave it to me. Finders keepers."

"*I'll* have that," Tracy snapped, grabbing the orb and stuffing it into her coat pocket, "and the two of you can shut up."

The two girls dropped their attitude before Tracy got angry.

"*Tracy Murphy!*" A voice was calling from the school parking lot.

"Who's that now?" Trish muttered, trying to make out the nicely dressed figure running toward them.

"It's that French teacher, what's-her-face. Orange," said Bev.

"Lemon," corrected Tracy. "And what the hell does she want?"

"Tracy Murphy," Ms. Lemon wheezed, gasping to catch her breath as she reached them. "I need to see you in my classroom immediately."

"Whatever it is, Miss, I didn't do it, and it doesn't matter anyway 'cause it's time to go home."

"I realize that, Tracy, but this is rather serious. I'm afraid you'll have to come with me."

"I don't have to go *anywhere*. I'm waiting for the bus."

Ms. Lemon's lips tightened, but none of the girls noticed the scared look in her eyes.

"Unless you'd like a month's detention, young lady," she said, "you'll come with me *right now*."

"Whatever," Tracy snarled, picking up her bag and following the teacher back to the main building.

"That's what she gets for stealing my paperweight," said Trish, as she and Bev watched them leave.

"It was *my* paperweight, and I'm telling her you said that," said Bev.

"Don't."

"What's it worth?"

"I'll give you back your paperweight."

"If Tracy gives it back to you?"

"Yeah."

"Okay."

✳✳✳

After the four girls had persuaded Ms. Lemon to detain the Beast in her classroom for her own safety, the search for the non-Una began in earnest. Block by block they checked each classroom, each toilet stall, and even each storage closet. As the sun began to set and the halls got darker, the school seemed emptier and scarier than it ever had before. Shadows bounced across the walls as the girls hurried from room to room, trying to ignore the sound of their footsteps in the eerie silence.

"This is taking too long," said Grace. "I think you're right, Jenny. We'll have to split up."

"Grace!" Adie said with a pained look.

"We *have* to, Adie. We're wasting time. Jenny, you and Rach head to the C block and work your way down. Me and Adie will go the opposite way and we'll meet in the middle."

"Okay." Jenny nodded.

"Scream if you see her."

"I'm sure we will," Rachel said over her shoulder as she trotted up the corridor after Jenny.

"Right, Adie, let's go," said Grace. "B block first."

"I hate this."

"I know."

The first two classrooms were empty and quiet. In the third, Grace absentmindedly ran her finger down the whiteboard, accidentally leaving inky fingermarks all over it, as she glanced around.

"And nothing here either," Grace sighed. "Girls' bathroom next."

She stood at the door watching as Adie nudged open each stall door. Her eyes drifted to the mirror on the opposite wall. There! There was definitely a reflection of a moving shadow beneath one of the doors.

"Adie! Wait—"

She was too late. The stall door flew open, smacking Adie on the cheek and sending her stumbling into the far wall. Before Grace could move, the non-Una had snatched Adie by the collar and bolted for the exit, jamming her elbow into Grace's chest as she ran. With blurred vision through watering eyes, Grace could just make out the two figures disappearing down the dim corridor before her winded lungs allowed her to scream.

"Jenny! *Rachel!*"

***

With panicked shouts Grace, Jenny, and Rachel thundered through rooms and corridors, knocking over chairs and tables as they pursued the non-Una.

"Oh God," breathed Rachel, "where have they gone?!"

"The P block," Jenny said suddenly. "Go. *Go!*"

Sprinting for all they were worth, they pushed through the double doors to the P block. They stopped dead and gasped at the horrible sight before them.

The non-Una knelt on the floor, pinning Adie to the ground with one hand and holding a triangular object in the other. A Ouija board lay unfolded beside her.

"No!" Jenny shrieked. Taking off at full speed, she slammed into the demon, letting her momentum carry both of them to the end of the hall where they crashed through the emergency exit, tumbling out into the open air. The non-Una let out a piercing screech and lunged for Jenny's throat, scratching her nails down Jenny's neck as she cemented her grip. Suddenly, Rachel was on top of her, grabbing her hair and pulling back with all her might. Adie and Grace scrambled from the building and joined the fight, but to no avail. Even with all three of the girls pulling at the non-Una's arms and pounding on her back, her grip on Jenny's throat wouldn't loosen. Jenny began to lose consciousness.

"Girls, I heard screaming—oh my *God*!"

"Ms. Lemon, *help* us!" shouted Grace.

The teacher snapped herself out of her shock, then pulled on a piece of string around her neck, revealing a small wooden charm. Lunging forward, she held the charm beneath the non-Una's nose and jumped back as the demon snorted loudly and leaped to her feet. All four girls were scattered across the ground as the demon stood snarling, her hot breath puffing out clouds of steam in the cool evening air.

The doorway to the P block crashed open again.

"Whatever's going on here," said a surly voice, "it's nothing to do with me, and I'm not—whoa!"

Tracy stopped at the doorway, taking in the sight before her. The fiendish-looking creature that resembled the girl she most liked to pick on had fiery red eyes, and its matted hair stood out from its head, framing a reddening face. As she watched, its canines sharpened and grew, and it pulled back its lips in a maniacal grin. Tracy whimpered.

"Where's the orb?" Ms. Lemon whispered urgently.

"I don't know," Grace cried in reply. "She doesn't have it."

Tracy edged along the wall. As the last bus of the day rounded the corner and turned into the school gates, she broke into a run.

"Tracy, no!" Adie took off after her as the others once again grabbed the non-Una. She fought back ferociously, tossing them aside one by one and cackling wickedly at their feeble efforts. Ms. Lemon took one hit and stumbled badly, banging her head against the open P block door. The non-Una hissed in delight as the teacher lost consciousness, then seized Grace by the hair and pulled her close.

"It's all over now," she growled.

Meanwhile, Adie was gaining on Tracy. She leaped onto her, gripping her jacket sleeve and spinning her around, just in time to see the school bus suddenly lose control and careen toward them at full speed. Tracy twisted around trying to shrug Adie off her back but fell backward instead. A navy-blue object bounced out of Tracy's pocket.

"Grace! *The orb!*" screamed Adie.

Grace looked up just as Adie scooped up the orb and flung it toward her friend. As it sailed through the air, Grace used every ounce of strength she had to launch herself from the demon's grip and reach to the sky. The orb glinted momentarily in the twilight and smacked right into Grace's palm.

"*Now!*" she screamed.

Like lightning, the enchanted ropes were flicked around the non-Una's wrists, and she was pulled to her knees. Grace sank to the ground and whispered the incantation.

> *"I curse you, Demon,*
> *Hound from hell!*
> *And banish you*
> *Back to the well!"*

The orb bounced out of her hands and exploded at Una's feet. A swirling mist erupted from it, encircling the non-Una in ever-decreasing spirals. It screamed as one fiery arm was pulled from Una's body, followed by the other. Its clawing fingers reached out to grab hold of Grace, but were immediately enveloped by a howling whirl of lost souls. The bus thundered toward Adie and Tracy, and the demon shrieked as it was wrenched from Una's body, finally revealing its wretched face, snapping at Jenny to its left and Rachel to its right with its hideous fangs. Within a split second its head was engulfed by screaming spirits as if they were drawn to it like moths to a flame. Adie jerked Tracy backward into a ditch, and the bus swept past them, missing them by a breath. The demon howled one long, last time as it was crushed beneath the awesome sound of the lost souls and disappeared into nothing.

***

"Ms. Lemon, are you all right?" said Grace.

"What? Are you…What's happened? Is it over?"

"Yep," said Grace, helping the teacher to her feet. "It's all over."

Una—the real Una—staggered toward Ms. Lemon, clutching Jenny's arm. She blinked and squinted, like a newborn baby seeing the world for the first time, and occasionally squeezed Jenny's arm with her free hand as if she couldn't possibly be real. Una's hair was standing out from her head, and her clothes were torn and disheveled. Grace couldn't help smiling—Una looked like she'd just stepped out of a washing machine set to spin.

"Hey," Una slurred, waving her arm loosely, "everybody's here. What's—ow!" Her hand flew to her face. "Ow! What the…?"

She ran her fingers over the emerging bruises on her cheeks, winced, then did the same to her ribs.

"Have you guys been beating me up?"

Rachel smoothed down Una's wild hair and gripped her in a hug that was a little too tight.

"We did," she said, blinking back tears. "But now that you're back, we promise not to beat you up anymore."

"It's really weird," said Una. "I can't remember much since we did the Ouija board that night in the P block—there's just blurry bits and pieces. It's so freaky."

Grace watched Una's pretty gray eyes and felt almost giddy with relief and happiness. When Rachel let go of her, she grabbed Una in a bear hug.

"Aw, stop with the hugging," Una groaned. "I'm sore all over."

Grace released her and kissed her bruised cheek. "We've missed you *so* much."

"That's nice, but, you know, be gentle about it.

Hey, do I have to thank you guys for saving me or something?"

"It's Grace you should thank. She did the worst part," said Adie, wrapping her arms very carefully around Una's neck. "It's so good to hear the real you again!"

"Where's Tracy?" Ms. Lemon said suddenly. "Is *she* all right?"

"Seems like it." Adie nodded toward the shaking figure slowly climbing out of the ditch. "Gave me a good punch in the stomach for my trouble too."

They all looked toward Tracy's cowering figure. She paused to stare at them with a mixture of venom and terror, before rushing onto the now-stationary bus.

"Shame," said Una, raising one eyebrow. "Looks like she got a good scare though."

"Una!" Ms. Lemon warned. Una looked contrite.

"So all our spells worked then?" she said after a moment.

"Except for that very last one, yeah," replied Grace.

"Does that mean that James O'Connor's in love

with you, Grace?" Una grinned, finally managing to stand by herself.

"Was. He won't be anymore."

"Not to worry. We'll do another one tomorrow."

"You will not!" Ms. Lemon snapped.

"We will not, Miss. You're absolutely right," Una said innocently, taking Adie and Rachel's hands and winking slyly. Grace grinned as Jenny threw an arm around Una's shoulder and squeezed.

"It's *so* good to have you back."

"Believe me—it's good to *be* back!"

***

The following morning, a bruise-covered Una walked up to the other girls as they stood by Grace's locker.

"So you all forgot to mention that you got me suspended," she said with a face like a bulldog.

"We did nothing of the sort," snapped Adie. "The *demon* got you suspended."

"Well," said Una, unimpressed, "it would appear I'm

still suffering from the fallout of that at home. I had to wash *and* dry the dishes last night, and Dad says I have to clean out the garage on Saturday. And when I complained he said, 'I thought you would understand how serious this was, because you've been behaving so well lately.' Ugh!"

"Oh, yeah," said Jenny, "the demon was a total teacher's pet. Everyone thinks you're a nerd now. Mr. Kilroy loves you."

"Ahh, stop! I don't want to hear any more!"

"Still," said Rachel cheerfully, "Tracy seems to have given you a wide berth this morning. Maybe the demon scared her off for good."

"Let's hope so," said Adie, picking up her bag. "Grace, are you coming?"

"I'll catch up," replied Grace, waving them off. "Just need to grab my math book."

Trotting over to her locker, she opened the door and dropped to her haunches with her bag just as the contents of her locker emptied, showering her in books. Tutting to herself, she threw them back in over her head and fastened her schoolbag again.

"You missed one."

"Oh, thanks," she said, taking the offered book without looking up.

"No problem. See you around, Grace."

She glanced up just in time to catch James O'Connor's warm smile before he turned and headed down the corridor. Slowly getting to her feet, she gazed at his retreating back, then smiled to herself. She pulled her bag onto her shoulder and hurried after her friends.

acknowledgments

I'd like to thank my mom, Eileen, for her endless love and support. And Oisín, Kunak, Marek, and Darius, because life is easy when you've always got people to lean on.

My editor, Marian Broderick, for sorting out my text and making a better book. To everyone at O'Brien Press, especially Susan Houlden for managing the project, and Emma Byrne for her brilliant design.

And a big thanks to my school friends who inspired this story—I promise I won't tell which parts are real and which are made up.

about the author

Erika McGann grew up in Drogheda, Ireland, and now lives in Dublin. She has a respectable job, very normal friends, and rarely dabbles in witchcraft. She loves writing stories that are autobiographical. Sort of.

The Demon Notebook is her first book.

Stay tuned for the next adventure in

The Broken Spell

Coming Fall 2014